What a cruel twist of fate!

Before Jane had found out Dirk's true identity her time with him had been a magical interlude, precious and fragile. But it had been shattered by the intrusion of the harsh reality of the past. As he was an orthopaedic surgeon at the very hospital where she worked, their paths were bound to cross. It was a damning irony. . .he was the only man in the world she couldn't let herself love!

Dear Reader

Practice Nurse Amy Kincaid finds that she is IN
SAFE HANDS in Margaret O'Neill's latest GP story,
while Canadian physiotherapist Jane Easter tries to
convince Dirk that the unknown can exist in Sara
Burton's BEYOND HEAVEN AND EARTH. A con-
valescent home is the unusual setting for Clare
Lavenham's offering in SISTER AT HILLSIDE, and
the beautiful Great Barrier Reef is the backdrop for
Judith Worthy's STORM IN PARADISE.

Travel the world without leaving home!

The Editor

Sara Burton was convent educated and trained as a
physiotherapist at a school in the Midlands. She has
worked in England, Scandinavia and North America,
and received her B.Sc. in Physical Therapy from a
Western Canada university. Currently she is
engaged in independent research related to partial
dislocations of joints in the lower limb. She is also a
bird-fancier, with special interest in homing pigeons.

Recent titles by the same author:

CAUGHT IN THE CROSSFIRE
HEART SEARCHING

BEYOND HEAVEN AND EARTH

BY

SARA BURTON

MILLS & BOON LIMITED
ETON HOUSE   18–24 PARADISE ROAD
RICHMOND   SURREY   TW9 1SR

First published in Great Britain 1992
by Mills & Boon Limited

© Sara Burton 1992

Australian copyright 1992
Philippine copyright 1992
This edition 1992

ISBN 0 263 77917 3

Set in 11 on 12½ pt Linotron Palatino
03-9211-41990

Typeset in Great Britain by Centracet, Cambridge
Made and printed in Great Britain

CHAPTER ONE

'HERE's your pearl. It rolled straight to me, so we must be fated to dance. . .*at least.*'

Jane had panicked when her antique string of pearls had suddenly broken. She had felt them sliding down her neck and had somehow managed to catch all but the one bead.

Now, here on the edge of the dance-floor in the Old-Timers' Cabin, she found herself staring down into the face of the man still crouching on the wooden floor.

His voice was low and vibrant and instantly caught at her heart-strings. And as he stood up to his full and impressive height she was unable to break her gaze.

'Thank you,' she murmured as he dropped the pearl into her palm. 'This necklace is very precious to me. It was a twenty-first brithday present from my father.'

'Then it's of great double value, because the beads have a fabulous lustre. . .a real inner light. And some feel the pearl symbolises the soul.'

The soft timbre to his words fascinated her. It seemed somehow at odds with his powerfully arresting, dark good looks. And to Jane he could have stepped straight from the wilderness of the nearby Rocky Mountains and hastily donned his white dinner-jacket and black dress trousers.

Fishing deep into his left trouser pocket, he produced a spotless white silk handkerchief. 'You've got nowhere to keep that broken necklace.' His glance roved over her long midnight-blue evening gown. For an instant it rested on her rounded breasts and cleavage. 'At least, nowhere where the bulge wouldn't spoil the cut of your dress.'

She blushed and tried to hide her smile. Such words from a stranger might have made her think the approach tacky, but this man's eyes crinkled into such a warm smile that she felt sincerely charmed. And fortune had certainly favoured him with the most brilliant emerald eyes she'd ever seen.

His deep voice continued to hold her spellbound. 'If I tie the pieces up in a neat parcel and keep it in my breast pocket, it'll be perfectly safe until you want to collect your evening coat and purse.'

She hesitated a moment before agreeing, then watched attentively.

His hands were strong yet remarkably deft, and he tied the little parcel with such precision that it looked almost elegant. Then he stowed it away, leaving only a tag of white silk peeping up.

'Your pearl introduced us. But, even if some people believe in the folklore and magic of gems, the pearl hasn't told me your name.'

'Jane. . .' she began.

'And I'm Dirk. Now we can dance.'

Instantly she found herself being pulled into his arms. He really had a silver tongue, but she knew she was falling under his spell quite happily.

Everything about him thrilled her senses. He appealed directly to her mind and to her body too. She could hardly believe her luck, especially as she had come to the dance by chance alone.

Jane Easter had moved from the next-door prairie province in Canada to start a new job as a physiotherapist in Outpatients at a general hospital near the Rockies. Today had been her first day of work, but the last one for the director of the rehabilitation unit who had given her the post.

She had felt almost exhausted by late afternoon and had only accepted the invitation to the rehab farewell out of a sense of duty. But, being a true believer in fate, Jane now accepted whole-heartedly that Dirk was to be a most important man in her life. The fates must have decreed it, othrwise why else was she here?

The band was playing a slow number, and Dirk held her close. For no reason she glanced up, and caught him looking into her eyes with such an intensity that her startled heart began to pound.

As if he was aware of this his fingers tightened around her hand and his eyes began to dilate darkly.

She had to know more about him. 'Where did you learn about gems and stones?' she asked.

His face immediately softened. 'My grandfather's passion was also his work. He was a jeweller. I often sat in silence and watched him cut stones. But most of the time, when he wasn't working so intensely, he would recite the little stories.'

He pulled her closer and spoke more softly, so that she could feel his warm breath against her ear.

'The band is excellent, but far too loud. Come with me on to the deck through these patio doors, then we can talk more comfortably.'

'I'd love to hear more of your grandfather's tales,' she told him.

Dirk's smile was disarming, and she knew she was being charmed, but he made her feel so alive that she would have followed him anywhere.

The late spring night was gorgeous and unseasonably warm. The stars studded the sky and a solitary wispy cloud split the moon. And to Jane the moon was shining more brilliantly than she had ever seen.

Now the music from the band was muffled

but still discernible. Far below in the ravine the river rushed headlong, and its noise floated gently up.

'My grandfather always thought the pearl most feminine,' he told her. 'In legend pearls are connected with the moon and water, so it's appropriate that we should dance here.'

Now that they were alone together and she was being pressed close up against Dirk, Jane felt a total energy shoot through her body. Everything was happening too fast; she had to slow it down or she would be in danger of losing all control. So she was almost relieved when he continued.

'Garnets are supposed to be lucky. The Hunzas of Kashmir made their bullets from them because they believed they'd be more harmful to their enemies.'

'I suppose the enemy welcomed stray shots,' she laughed.

Dirk grinned and chuckled too. Then he held her slightly away. 'If you'd lived long ago in the Middle Ages a ruby ring worn on your left hand would have protected you against seduction.'

After inspecting her bare left fingers for some time he lifted his gaze slowly and asked huskily, 'Are you open to se——?'

Jane cut him off swiftly. 'Open to *suggestion*— in time, perhaps.'

Dirk smiled knowingly. 'More fairy-tales first for entertainment, I suppose.'

'The way you tell your stories tells me a lot about you,' she said.

'Hmm. . . I'm racking my brain hard.' He sounded teasing. 'The Romans thought amethysts prevented drunkenness. Some even placed the stones in their goblets of wine, really believing in the myth.'

She looked at him warily for an instant.

'Don't fret,' he continued seriously. 'I wouldn't dream of suggesting we try the myth out. My intentions are all honourable, and a woman who's three sheets in the wind doesn't appeal to me.'

Jane swallowed hard. The conversation was bordering on the outrageous. She must be mad to go along with this man's banter. He was smoothly seductive.

Before she could think of a suitable reply she was pressed hard against the full length of his body, and his first kiss was so swift that it sent a quiver through her heart. Parting her lips slightly, almost as much in surprise as anything else, was her undoing. Dirk's kisses were deep and probing. The sweet sensation made her feel physically weak, and the touch of his tongue on hers awakened a response that she had never given to any man in her life before.

Dirk was so entertaining and exciting, she wanted more of him, so she kissed him back with the fierce passion that matched his.

The sound of a discreet cough brought her

back to earth, and she tore her lips from Dirk's. He on the other hand continued to hold her captive.

'Excuse me for interrupting, sir.' The young waiter looked slightly embarrassed. 'But there's an urgent telephone call for you in Reception.'

'Thanks. I'll follow you directly.' Dirk's reply was almost curt, but it had the required effect as the waiter made a rapid exit.

'I think I know the problem,' Dirk began to explain. 'With luck, I can sort it out on the phone.' He sighed and slowly relinquished his hold. Then he tugged the handkerchief from his pocket. 'If I have to go back to the hospital, I may be there for several hours, so you'd better have your pearls now.'

'If you can't stay on here, then I'll understand.' Jane tried to keep the disappointment from her voice. The very idea of being away from him for even a few minutes now would feel like a wrench.

As she cluthed her necklace he covered her hands with his. 'Wait for me here; I'll do my damnedest to come back.'

His kiss was too fleeting for her liking, and suddenly he was gone, striding purposefully through the crowds on the dance-floor.

When he was finally out of sight, Jane turned her gaze to the split moon. That man makes my toes curl, she thought. Yes, she had fallen head over heels in love, and what was even more brilliant about the situation was her true belief that Dirk felt exactly the same.

Moments later the young waiter returned, and Jane groaned inwardly. Obviously Dirk was needed urgently elsewhere.

'Dr Blackwell's very sorry, ma'am, but he's been summoned back to the general hospital for an emergency.'

Jane's breath caught in her throat and she stared at the waiter incredulously. It wasn't the content of the message but the doctor's name that had so startled her.

Misinterpreting her reactions, the waiter continued more gently, 'Dr Blackwell was very upset about leaving you, ma'am. But he's left his phone number on this piece of paper.' He handed it over, and Jane took it reluctantly.

'Just ring the doctor at his home in a few hours and I'm sure your night won't have ended so abruptly.'

'Th—thank you,' she stammered. Then, 'Wait. . . Do you know if *this* Dr Blackwell comes from Saskatchewan, and if his father's a cardiologist?'

The young man smiled as if he had good news. 'Yes, I believe he's from that province, and his father's a doctor too. It's lucky I know, because my mate had his shoulder treated by Dirk Blackwell only a few days ago. He's a damn fine orthopaedic surgeon.'

Feeling her heart plummet at the news almost

made Jane cry, but she had just enough control
to thank the waiter and pull herself together.

When she was alone in the night air, on the
deck, painful images from the past enveloped
her mind. Her father had suffered from a rare
cardiac condition, and a Dr Blackwell had treated
him. Although her father's treatment couldn't
be faulted from a medico-science point of view,
Jane had frequently pestered the cardiologist
because she'd believed her father's condition
was more critical. But she had had nothing more
to go on than a heavy gut feeling, so the
cardiologist had always told her not to fuss.

But all her instincts had told her that something disastrous would happen. She had even
let her father know that if he died she would
hold Dr Blackwell responsible and she would
pursue him.

He father's response had been adamant to all
this. He had told Jane that if he died it would
be at the hands of fate and fate alone, and he'd
charged her to forget all thoughts of revenge
because they would only hurt her in the long
run.

Her father had died only weeks later, the
result of an unforeseen complication, according
to Dr Blackwell, the cardiologist. But according
to Jane, his death was due to a doctor who
wouldn't listen.

However, all this had been over a year ago,

and until now Jane had successfully repressed
all thoughts of revenge.

Her eyes misted over. What a cruel twist of
fate to make her fall in love with the man she
believed to be the son of the doctor who had
been responsible for the cause of her father's
death!

Before she had found out Dirk's true identity
her time with him had been a magical interlude,
precious and fragile. But it had been shattered
by the intrusion of the harsh reality of the past.

Reluctantly she threw his note towards the
dark recess of the deep ravine. As he was an
orthopaedic surgeon at the very hospital where
she worked, their paths were bound to cross. It
was a damning irony. . .he was the only man
in the world she couldn't let herself love!

By the following working day Jane had just
about come down from the shock and surprise
of the revelations from the night of the dance.

She always took care to look professional for
work, but today she had made an extra effort.
Now she wore no make-up and she had drawn
her long dark hair well off her face and secured
it with a tortoiseshell slide at the nape of her
neck.

Her Wedgwood-blue eyes, flecked with
ebony, were distinctive, she knew, but without
the skilful make-up that she had worn when
she first met Dirk it might be possible to pass

him in a corridor and still remain unrecognised.
And she had been pleased to hear from her
workmates that he rarely put in an appearance
in the physiotherapy department. Most of his
communications came through writing in the
form of requisitions or over the phone.

However, Jane had no time to dwell on Dirk.
One of her patients was posing a problem. Tom
Gulliver hadn't turned up for his physio
appointments, either for Jane or the physio
whose post Jane had taken over.

A few months ago the lad of sixteen had
raced his mountain bike so rapidly down a hill
that he'd lost control of the machine, and
crashed into a tree.

His head injury had been fairly severe and he
had spent a couple of weeks unconscious in
hospital.

On regaining consciousness he had made a
rapid recovery and now had only residual problems with speech and a few memory dysfunc-
tions. His present referral for physio was for a
shoulder problem.

Although the lad was under Dirk Blackwell's
care, a junior doctor had examined him and
ordered this treatment. The only information
Jane had on the requisition read, 'Painful
shoulder. Physio treatment.'

As Tom was only sixteen, Jane had opted to
ring the mother and talk to her. Mrs Gulliver
sounded harassed, to say the least. 'It's a bit

difficult to bring Tom in this afternoon,' she explained. 'Everyone's busy here in the house. And he's not capable of managing the journey on his own.'

'Could a friend or neighbour bring him?' Jane enquired.

There was no immediate reply, and Jane could understand why. A cacophony of babies bawling assailed her ears, then she could hear Mrs Gulliver trying to soothe them, only to be interrupted by the gruff shout of a man's command.

Finally the mother came back to the phone and spoke with desperation. 'Well, somebody's got to do something about Tom—he just sits about the house clutching his arm. He's making everyone miserable. I'll try and get the old man next door to bring him.'

'Would three o'clock be suitable?' There was a silence. 'But any time before five would do.'

'Yes, yes,' replied the mother. 'I'm sure our neighbour will bring him.'

They said their goodbyes and rang off.

At three o'clock precisely, as Jane was stowing away some sandbags from a previous patient, she saw an elderly man and a lad enter the waiting area. The older man behaved very attentively to his charge, and took time to see that he was settled comfortably on one of the bench seats before he hurried away.

Now there's my patient Tom, thought Jane.

And she took advantage of the opportunity to study him. The lad sat hunched forward, gripping his right arm tightly to his side. His head hung down and his lower lip jutted out. His curly hair was in need of a cut and it hung down well over his forehead. But the thing that struck Jane most forcibly was the fact that this youngster looked as if he were under a sentence of death.

She walked up and gently asked if his name was Tom Gulliver. He nodded his head as if dumb, so she spoke reassuringly.

'I'm your physiotherapist, Jane Easter. Come with me and we can set about fixing your shoulder.'

He stood up almost like an automaton and followed her into a treatment cubicle.

'Slip off your coat and shirt, please, Tom,' said Jane.

The lad removed his clothes gingerly, taking great care to protect his right arm all the while.

When he was undressed above the waist, Jane said, 'Sit on the plinth while I take some notes.'

Still without speaking, he climbed on to the high plinth and stared mutely at the floor. Jane noticed that his hair was greasy and flecked with dandruff. He really was in a very unkempt condition.

'Now, Tom,' she began gently, 'did you injure your shoulder when you hurt your head?'

'No,' he replied without looking up.

'Then how did you injure it?'

'It just came on. A week ago.'

'Did you wake up and find you had the pain suddenly one morning?' Jane continued to probe.

'I don't know,' he answered wearily.

Further direct questions got her no further forward, so she pocketed her notepad and pencil and decided to go straight on to the clinical examination. She tried to coax Tom to move his arm actively, but he couldn't seem to move it more than a few inches away from his body in any direction. And as the examination continued she became more perplexed. He seemed to have no particular pain anywhere, and yet his muscles were quite strong when he was asked to do an isometric muscle contraction. During the isometric test she felt all his shoulder muscles contract quite powerfully while she held his arm by his side.

Next she wondered if his scapula or shoulder-blade had been injured, and whether it was now adherent to the soft tissues near his rib-cage. But when he lay on his tummy she found that she could move the scapula very easily through its full range of motion. And through all other ranges she could passively move his arm.

It was becoming clearer and clearer to Jane that Tom's shoulder problem might be of an hysterical origin. The home situation had certainly sounded dicey over the phone. Perhaps Tom just wanted attention.

When she had completed her examination Jane sat by her patient on the plinth. She decided to take a positive but firm, optimistic approach.

'I think exercise will play an important part in your treatment, Tom. But you'll have to make quite an effort yourself.'

'There's no point,' he answered slowly in his hesitant monotone speech.

'Why not?' she intervened quickly, wishing to dispel any thoughts of negativity.

'Because I've had the voodoo put on me.'

This answer so shocked Jane that her eyebrows nearly rose up to her hairline. But one look at Tom's face told her that wherever the boy had got this incredible idea it had sunk home, because he really believed in it.

Quelling the surprise in her voice, she asked, 'Where was this voodoo put on you?'

'I was playing with some guys on a building site, and then some of them laughed at me, and put it on me. Just over on Vancouver Island.'

On the Island, Jane repeated in her thoughts. 'Well, then, there's no need for you to worry any more, Tom, because the voodoo can't cross the water,' she told him.

She had no idea why she had said this. All she knew was that it had the most amazing and instantly transforming effect. The lad turned quickly and gaped straight at her, his eyes wide with expectancy.

Seeing that she had hit a responsive chord, Jane repeated, 'That's right—the voodoo cannot cross the water.'

This second statement seemed to sink deep, because his face lit up. 'Oh, I didn't know that.'

Jane pressed on, 'However, I think there's a little stiffness and weakness left in your shoulder. And it'll take a few white-coat magic treatments to make you fit again.'

Tom sat up straight and a faint smile began to play around the corners of his lips and his eyes. 'Yes, I'll do just what you say. White-coat magic . . .that's the stuff for me all right.'

This is a piece of luck, thought Jane. I'm on a winning streak here. 'We'll start with a nice soothing moist heat pack. I'll go and prepare that for you, Tom. Now you just lie back on the plinth and relax until I come back.'

He looked delighted at this idea, and Jane was even more pleased with herself as she stepped out from the cubicle and walked towards the hydrocolater.

But her rising good spirits were immediately quashed when her elbow was taken in a vicelike grip and she found herself being propelled towards the empty outpatients office.

'I want a word with you, young lady. And in private!'

Jane would have known *that* voice anywhere. It was Dirk Blackwell. And he sounded thoroughly annoyed.

She was marched into the office in double-quick time. After shutting the door firmly, Dirk turned and stood before her with his arms folded across his chest.

'What in God's name are you doing with my patient Tom Gulliver? As I walked through the department I could hear you filling the lad's mind with white magic and hocus-pocus.'

He raced on, not giving her a chance to reply, 'I don't know where you trained, but here at the General my patients are treated with a sense of the realities. And that means purely on scientific facts!'

CHAPTER TWO

DR DIRK BLACKWELL's tone was only slightly tempered now. But he still spoke with a steely invective.

'I find this sort of talk particularly irritating, and downright dangerous.'

The way his black eyebrows were lowered formidably above his eyes left Jane in no doubt that he meant exactly what he said.

He continued without drawing breath, 'In fact, my very reason for coming to visit your new director was associated with fringe medicine.'

Jane could see that Dirk was suppressing some sort of rage. She continued to listen as if on tenterhooks, because his mind was obviously clouded with this problem, and he hadn't recognised her yet.

'One of my colleagues' patients has just died at the hands of some quack, some "chiropractor" who wasn't remotely qualified. The patient had a fear of doctors and injections in particular, so when he was diagnosed diabetic he went for treatment with this "chiropractor".'

Dirk's eyes flashed. 'The patient was told that manipulating the spine could cure diabetes. Of course the treatment didn't work, the condition went out of control and the outcome was fatal!'

'That's a grim story,' Jane commented. 'But my method of dealing with Tom's problems stems from the fact that the lad really believes a voodoo has been put on him.'

Dirk didn't seem to be comprehending; his mind was obviously still turning on the unfortunate diabetes patient.

'Madam,' he continued severely, 'don't feed my patients any mumbo-jumbo at all. With your way of thinking you'll be directing them to the nearest demonstration of crystal-ball healing——'

'Excuse me, sir,' she butted in, rebellion getting the better of her.

'No! Listen to me.' His authoritative voice drowned her out. 'My patients are to be treated with medical science and scientific fact alone.'

Now Jane was furious that he wouldn't listen, and that he wasn't giving her a chance to explain the facts. Her mind flashed back to the arguments she had had with Dr Blackwell the cardiologist. And now at this moment Dirk was behaving exactly like his father. Gritting her teeth, she tried desperately to stabilise her feelings.

'What's your name, young lady?' Dirk contemptuously tilted her name tag with the tip of his right finger. 'Jane Easter. . . Ja——'

His words stopped in mid-sentence, and he

stared at her incredulously. 'Jane? But it's you
. . .you. . . Why must it be you arguing with
me about this contentious point?'

Now he had recognised her, it was as if her
heart stood still. After a moment's hesitancy she
continued, 'I'm *trying* to put my points across.'

Her mind was in such a turmoil that she
could see Dirk's arrogant features soften as he
recognised her. A look almost like pain
shrouded his eyes. The subject of the patient
seemed to be forgotten temporarily.

'I sent my phone number to you last night,
Jane. It was the only thing I could do in the
circumstances, because I was needed here. And
you know, I stayed awake all through the night
waiting for your call.'

Jane couldn't bear to look in his eyes. Not
wanting to explain the whole scenario surrounding her father's death, she turned away.

Then she replied quickly with the first thing
that came into her head. 'If you say you sent a
note, then I suppose you sent it.'

'Damn that waiter,' Dirk muttered under his
breath. 'I expect he didn't make any attempt to
find you.'

Jane continued to avert her eyes because the
whole situation was way beyond her liking.
Then, with a sudden halt on her emotions, she
went on, 'Let's get back to this misunderstanding about Tom Gulliver and the voodoo. And,

if you'd just let me explain, I am trying to treat the lad using scientific reasoning.'

She took a deep breath. 'There've been substantiated reports of voodoo influences. They're written up in the *Journal of Psychsomatic Medicine*, and examples have come from South America, Africa and Australia. I think the lad's shoulder problem is entirely caused by the fact that some stupid and ignorant people have put this idea into his head. And, because his intellectual functions aren't one hundred per cent following his injury, he's credulous and has believed it.'

'Dr Blackwell to Emergency. Dr Blackwell to Emergency. . .stat!' The untimely summons came urgently over the intercom, and Dirk immediately jerked his head in that direction as if to listen.

His expression was one of near-exasperation. 'Have dinner with me tonight, Jane. I can pick you up directly you finish work. Many things must be sorted out between us.'

'I'm sorry, sir.' She tried to sound detached. 'But I've already got something planned.'

'Tomorrow night, then.' He sounded desperate.

The intercom interrupted once more.

'I'm sorry, but that's not possible either,' said Jane.

He looked at her darkly, and studied her face so intently that she felt her hands begin to tremble.

'Book Tom Gulliver into my physio clinic next week so that I can examine him properly, Jane. But in the meantime remember this.' His stern expression was dominant now. 'If you must persist in this white-magic-treatment line, bear in mind. . . Me doctor, you Jane. So all my patients must be treated along medico-science paths. And secondly. . .' He hesitated before walking out. 'I really did send that note for you. I wanted you that night, just as much as I believed you wanted me.'

With those words he was gone, leaving Jane feeling thoroughly annoyed, thoroughly upset and definitely confused. It would be easier if she could just dislike the man. His parting words had come from his heart; she felt sure about that. If only he weren't the son of *that* cardiologist!

After a moment's reflection the full force of their current argument came back into her mind. Searching the notice board, she found that Dirk's next physio clinic was only a week away. Precious little time in which to treat and completely cure Tom Gulliver.

Time certainly wasn't on her side, but she was damn well going to do it, and prove that instinct together with intellectual scientific treatment could bring about a better result.

As she stepped back out into the department she remembered that she hadn't tested Tom for hot and cold sensation on the skin of his shoulder. So she collected two empty test-tubes, and filled one with hot water and the other with ice from the ice machine.

Glancing up at the clock, she realised that she'd been away from Tom for quite some time. She hoped he hadn't been fretting about anything. But when she re-entered the cubicle she was greeted with the brightest of smiles.

'I'm sorry I've taken so long, but I had to discuss a patient with a doctor,' she told him.

'Sure, that's fine by me. I knew you'd come back.'

Jane was impressed with the complete and utter trust that the lad now displayed for her. A good thing too, she thought.

Fortunately Tom could distinguish between the hot and cold test-tube, and he could understand the warning about getting a burn from the hot pack, if it should feel too hot.

Then she returned to the sink by the hydrocolater, and after emptying the test-tubes stored them back on their rack. The hot packs that contained a Fuller's earth material were stored in hot water. Using the tongs, she fished one out and set it on one of the previously prepared towels.

Taking care, she folded in the tags and arranged the pack in more towels. Then she made her patient comfortable with pillows and gave him a bell to ring in case the treatment got too hot.

She was about to return to the nearby office to write up her notes when the elderly gentleman who had escorted Tom into the department walked up to her.

'Excuse me, ma'am, but are you the physio who's looking after young Tom Gulliver?'

'Yes.' She introduced herself, then asked, 'Are you his next-door neighbour?'

'Uncle Chuck, ma'am.' They shook hands. 'That's what I like everyone to call me. I'm only too willing to help out when anyone's got a problem.' He hesitated a moment. 'Could I have a quiet word with you, please?'

'Of course.' Jane was keen to learn more about Tom's background, so she led Uncle Chuck into an empty area outside the main secretaries' office.

He was a kindly and impressive-looking man. He wore his baseball cap tilted way back on his close-shaven head. And, judging by the white colour of the bristles on his chin, Jane guessed he had retired from working life.

Concern clouded the older man's face. 'I'm worried about the lad. You see, there's a problem at home.'

Jane motioned to a couple of chairs, then sat down.

Uncle Chuck continued, 'His mum's having a hard time at the moment. Tom's father took a hike some years ago, and he never bothered to come back for the lad. And then Mrs Gulliver took up with another man, and now she's got her hands full with the little babies. Unfortunately, the man isn't too keen on Tom, especially since the lad's accident.'

Jane nodded encouragingly. But inside she was worried. It looked as if Tom was not only going to have to deal with the shock and physical adjustments following his injuries, together with the voodoo viciousness, but a fractured family situation as well.

'I'll bring the lad any time he needs treatment,' went on Uncle Chuck. 'And I'll do anything to help, but I feel at such a loss. I suppose it's because it's the poor lad's *head* that got the knock. Is that the reason for the shoulder problem now?'

Now Jane was in a professional dilemma. It wasn't really correct to discuss the patient with a stranger. But then Tom's home situation was particularly difficult, and Uncle Chuck here might be the very man to pull the lad through.

Not wanting to bring up the voodoo because of the roasting she had just had with Dirk, she had to choose her next words very carefully.

'I think Tom's shoulder problem isn't too severe. I'm optimistic that it'll clear up fairly quickly as long as he comes for regular treatment.'

'Ah, that's something,' nodded Uncle Chuck. 'But, you know, he isn't quite the same lad that he used to be. Since he banged his head his memory and his intelligence seem to have suffered. For a start, he can't remember riding his bike and crashing into the tree.'

'That's quite common,' explained Jane. 'Retrograde amnesia is the medical term. Patients frequently can't recall the events immediately preceding the injury. It's not a significant problem in itself; some authorities believe it's due to the disturbance of short-term memory before it's encoded into long-term memory.'

'I think I can follow that,' he said slowly. 'But will he ever be as good as he was before the accident? He used to be such a bright lad.'

Jane spoke reassuringly. 'Tom's young, he's still a teenager. His chances of a complete recovery are very good, much more so than if he was over the age of forty. Also, following head injury, memory and intellect can recover at different times. I think it's early days yet, but he does need as much support as possible. And I think your help will be invaluable.'

'Does that mean his slow speech will get better too?' Uncle Chuck had brightened visibly.

'I hope so,' said Jane guardedly. It was a mistake to promise too much when it came to any patient's recovery.

'You see, when he's talking now he seems a bit dim.' The man's forehead crinkled. 'And I think he gets quite a bit of teasing about that.'

'Yes, that's totally unfair,' condemned Jane.

'But, as I said, it's early days yet. Perhaps you'd like to come and sit with Tom while he's on his moist heat treatment? And then, when I go through his exercises with him, you can give him some moral support.'

'Sure thing,' Uncle Chuck beamed.

Jane led the way into Tom's cubicle. 'I've got a visitor for you,' she smiled.

Uncle Chuck greeted the lad, then sat on one of the wooden chairs and made himself comfortable.

'This is really great,' Tom told the older man. 'I can feel this moist heat doing me good already.' He looked back at Jane, and not only was there a sweetness in the tone of his voice now, but also a real look of hope.

Spotting this too, Uncle Chuck said, 'Amazing! Jane must know what she's doing, because you look better already.'

They all laughed together, and Jane made her way back to the outpatients office.

'You look pleased with yourself.' Graham Walker, the only male physio in the department, looked up from his bench where he was reading an anatomy textbook.

Although about the same age as Jane— twenty-three—he looked more mature than his years. This was probably due to the fact that he had married during his student days and now had two youngsters to support.

'Yes,' Jane laughed softly. 'I think I'm well on

the way to curing a patient who's had a voodoo put on him.'

'I think that needs some sort of an explanation.' Graham looked astonished.

He pulled out another high stool and Jane sat down beside him. She recounted Tom's history and his confession about the cause of his shoulder problem. And when she came to the part about the voodoo not being able to cross the water she sounded quite elated.

'Clever girl!' congratulated Graham as he stroked his chin. 'The power of the mind is a force to be reckoned with. We shouldn't forget that. I've no doubt your patient will make a rapid recovery, but what made you think of those particular words?'

For a moment Jane was at a loss, then she suddenly remembered. 'When I took anthropology as one of my electives at university, our prof gave a lecture on the subject of voodoo. He mentioned some vivid examples, and I suppose that old information stored in my mind all those years ago suddenly helped me out.'

'Who's Tom's referring doctor?' he asked.

Jane's face fell. 'Dirk Blackwell.'

'That's a piece of luck. He's keen to write up his successes in the medical journals. And this will be a real feather in the cap for Physio.'

'It ought to be,' Jane rejoined hesitantly. 'But we've had a misunderstanding about the whole event, and he isn't fully conversant with exactly what happened.' She explained the circumstances in more detail, but carefully omitted the strong emotional undercurrent.

'I wouldn't worry,' said Graham. 'Blackwell will see the results for himself in clinic.'

'Thanks for your vote of confidence.' Jane decided she liked Graham; there was something soothingly reassuring about him.

When Tom's treatment time on the hot pack was over, he sat up eagerly. Jane knew it would be a temptation to advance his treatment too rapidly, so she decided to give him only a few simple exercises today. And she was careful to explain the significance of the range of motion exercises to both her patient and Uncle Chuck, and she advised Tom to repeat the regime again later that evening.

Then, after arranging another appointment for the following day, she waved them goodbye.

Back in the outpatients office Graham replaced the receiver on the telephone. 'Your eight o'clock patient has been discharged from the clinic,' he told her. 'You'd better wipe his name off your timetable on the board.'

'I'll do that right now,' she said and, taking a tissue, she moistened it with cleaning fluid, then stood on a chair to reach the top of the board.

Just then Claire Jousserand, the director, entered the office. 'Now there's a piece of luck.

How would you like a new patient for postural correction, Jane?'

'Fine; he can have this early empty slot. What's his name?'

'Boyd Harvey.'

Jane wrote the name in capitals in the space.

Claire continued, 'Come with me and I'll give you all the details. This is a little unusual, but I think physio will be able to play an important role here.'

In the director's office Jane waited while Claire finished a conversation on the phone. 'Yes, Jane Easter will be treating the young man. That's right, eight o'clock tomorrow. Goodbye.'

The new director handed some scribbled notes across her desk. 'The head of Psychiatry has referred this guy to us because he needs to be stretched a couple of centimetres. . . The reason Boyd needs to gain height is that he hasn't got the minimum height required to enter the police.'

'The Royal Canadian Mounted Police, eh?' Jane had a mental image of the huge hunks of men dressed in their impressive red tunics.

'Just the ordinary force,' Claire explained. 'Apparently this has always been this guy's dream.' Leaning back in her swivel chair, she tapped her fingertips with her pen. 'Initially, I had reservations about accepting this referral. But posture of the spine has great clinical significance. And a faulty posture can lead to all sorts of medical problems later on in life.'

Jane agreed.

Claire continued, 'So, I'm viewing this situation as a piece of prophylactic physiotherapy.'

'Young men and women were referred to one of the hospitals in the east where I did my interning for just this reason,' Jane told her.

'Tell me more.' Claire leaned forward across her desk.

'It was easy to gain the height for one young man because he had a slouch. And then with the woman they finally got the extra centimetres by traction. In fact, it was a great palaver, because the day she went for her medical examination with the police she was taken on a stretcher straight from her bed, given traction, transferred on to the stretcher again and rushed to the police. She only stood up that morning to be measured.'

'Ah, yes, of course.' Claire looked quite fascinated. 'The intervertebral discs would have been wider first thing in the morning before she took weight through her spine. They wouldn't have had any compressive forces on them.'

'Exactly,' Jane agreed.

'I think our old director made a very shrewd move when he took you on the staff, Jane,' Claire told her.

By the time Jane left Claire's office she felt

pretty buoyed up. And that business with Dirk had been completely forgotten.

But Boyd Harvey's treatment would prove to be a series of troubles. The first one started just as Jane was packing up to leave for the day, when his aunt phoned.

The older woman had a slightly superior condescending voice. 'Would it be possible, my dear, to change Boyd's appointment time? Eight o'clock is so frightfully early in the morning. And I've heard that the traffic at that time is murderous, and parking at the hospital almost a nightmare.'

Jane had to take a firm stand right from the start. 'It wouldn't be possible, because Boyd needs to be measured very early in the morning when his body height is at its tallest.' She continued to explain as simply as possible about the compressive forces on the discs, and how this could actually decrease height.

'Oh, dear, oh, dear,' came the laconic reply down the phone. 'I can see you've got a point there. Poor Boyd is so nervous about this whole affair. It's because it's his dream to enter the force.' The older woman's voice took on a sweetly commanding tone now. 'Boyd's father holds a very high rank in the police in one of the prairie provinces, and Boyd just longs to follow in his footsteps.'

Refusing to be swayed at all, Jane emphasised, 'But eight o'clock is the very best time, otherwise the treatment may fail.'

'Oh, it mustn't fail. Boyd's father always gets what he wants. I'll drive him to the hospital myself.'

On the more practical side Jane added, 'Please make sure that he brings a pair of cut-offs or something similar, because when I examine his posture he should be stripped down as far as possible.'

'I'll pack those for him myself. Thank you, you've been very kind to explain everything so fully.'

After saying goodbye, Jane had a few doubtful thoughts. If Boyd Harvey's one ambition was to become a policeman, and if he wished to excel, then why hadn't he made that simple phone call himself?

She shrugged and forgot all about it until the next morning, when one of the secretaries announced Boyd Harvey's arrival over the intercom.

As soon as Jane saw her patient her first thought was, Oh, dear! I haven't got a lot of leeway to increase his height, because he's standing very upright naturally.

After making the introductions she led the way to a cubicle. She noticed that his body was lean, and he didn't carry much weight.

'Are you wearing swimming-trunks or something under your jeans?' she enquired.

'No,' came the curious reply. 'Oh, no! I left my cut-offs in my aunt's car—I'm sorry.'

'Don't worry about it today, I can get you some disposable swimwear from the hydrotherapy section.'

When Boyd had changed into the trunks, Jane led him into the gym so that she could take some specific measurements. She made him stand against the special posture equipment that was used for measuring spinal defects.

'Stand as tall as you can now,' she ordered, and watched as he made the fault of tilting his head backwards. As he did this he also exaggerated the lordosis or lumbar curve near the base of his spine. 'Hmm. . .' murmured Jane as she brought the measuring rod down. 'You're just over two centimetres short of the mark.'

Boyd's response sounded disgruntled. 'If only I'd grown more during the time Dad sent me away to university.'

'Let's concentrate on the present situation.' Jane spoke calmly. 'You're actually losing height by exaggerating the curves in your neck and lower back.' She pointed this out as he stood next to a full-length wall mirror.

Then, placing her fingertips towards the back of his head, she instructed, 'Push upwards against the pressure of my hand. In that way you'll straighten out the curves. . . That's better; you've gained a centimetre already.'

Boyd was ecstatic. 'I knew this would work, I

knew it! My dad had to pull a lot of strings to get me in for this treatment—a mean doctor here wouldn't refer me. But Dad always gets what he wants.'

Jane was shocked at the hostility in Boyd's voice, but she could see that joining the police was of great importance to him.

Completely straightening out the lumbar curve proved difficult for him to grasp. 'Try and relax as much as possible,' she advised. 'I know that's difficult, but you can see these massive muscles running down your back, and if they're in a state of permanent tension and contraction then they'll compress your spinal system.'

'I just can't get the idea of this pelvic tilt.' He sounded frustrated.

So Jane had to bodily manhandle him, and litrally push him into the correct position. 'This is the correct posture; now try and hold it.'

After much effort he managed to maintain the posture and gained a little more height.

Jane recalled the example of the policewoman she had seen treated. This seemed to give Boyd a real boost, so he was very enthusiastic to follow her to the traction area, which was to one side of the gym.

'It's just like one of those medieval torture racks,' he laughed as she strapped in first the thoracic and then the lumbar belts.

'Not *quite* the same,' she quipped. 'This won't hurt.'

She set him up for an initial treatment of twenty minutes at an intermittent pull, and when he seemed settled she sat at the nearby desk to make notes. Frequently she glanced up to check him and was pleased to see that he looked elated.

After the session she relaxed the harnesses but advised, 'It's best if you lie here for twenty minutes. I've got another patient due, so I'll come back for you.'

As she passed from the gym into the general treatment area, she was engrossed in thoughts about gaining more height for Boyd, so she didn't hear Dirk Blackwell's first call. But when his deep voice did penetrate her heart skipped a beat.

'Are you on cloud nine or something, Jane? I had to call twice.' He looked disapprovingly down from his lofty height.

'I'm sorry, Dr Blackwell, I was considering a patient.'

Looking across at the traction, he began without preamble, 'Am I mistaken, or is that young Boyd here?'

'Yes, he's my patient,' she replied evenly, not understanding the reason for his sombre expression.

'No doubt his father has inveigled him here so that he can be stretched to the minimum height for the police.'

'He's been referred quite legally, and by the

head of Psychiatry.' She felt she needed to justify her part. 'In fact, Claire Jousserand did have some ethical misgivings, but after careful reflection she decided that prophylactic correction of his posture would prevent problems later in life.'

'Whatever the rationale, I thoroughly disapprove of that boy being here in Physio using our facilities for nothing more than career advancement!' he said stiffly.

Jane held her breath. Obviously Dirk was the 'mean' doctor whom Boyd had spoken of.

'The boy's whole mental attitude is wrong for the force,' he went on. 'During the short time I examined him, his only thoughts were about the power and the money that the job would bring.'

She gulped.

Dirk continued, 'Even after training, I can't see him comforting the bereaved at the scene of an MVA. Or indeed picking up the arms and legs of suicides from the railway track. He's psychologically immature, and if he didn't grow up during the three years he was at university then he never will.'

The doctor's hard-hitting imagery was brutal, but Jane knew that the police faced such scenes every day in their jobs.

'Apart from his mental incapacity, he's physically not up to the job either. The police need to be tall and beefy with it when they're handling incidents of disorder. For a start, a superior height and physique can have an intimidating effect, and this in itself can prevent trouble.'

He was in full flow now; there was no stopping him.

'When I consider police injuries I feel that my attitude is totally correct. On the lighter side they receive kicks in the groin and broken jaws, but in a riot situation that's a different matter. If you're small and weak you can easily lose your footing and fall. Then the crowd can surge and trample you down, and the result can be fatal.'

Jane shuddered inside and could only repeat, 'But he's been referred by the head of Psychiatry.'

'That's a branch of medicine where the theories aren't sufficiently substantiated by rigorous scientific research.'

Dirk paused, then looked wearily at Jane. 'Well, I only hope Boyd isn't taking valuable treatment time away from my patients.'

'Rest assured, your patients aren't suffering,' she told him.

'I'll check that out for myself in clinic next week, where the facts will speak for themselves!'

Their mutual hostile goodbye left Jane feeling that the man was clinical and cynical. On a moonlit magic night she had thought him devastatingly attractive. How wrong could she have been?

CHAPTER THREE

IT WAS ten-twenty the following morning, and Jane was sitting alone in the office as most of the other staff had gone up to the canteen.

Suddenly she looked up straight into the eyes of the man who most disturbed her. Caught off guard, she was annoyed to feel her heart lurch.

'Could you possibly treat one of my patients straight away, please, Jane? Harry Adamski's had a run of bad luck, and I'm afraid a real depression might set in if we don't start his rehab right away.'

Ah, now Dirk's putting on the charm because he wants something, she thought. But, whatever her feelings for the man, the patient came first.

'Of course. What's Harry's problem?' she asked.

Dirk set the pink requisition on top of the bench before her. 'I'd better give you his past history so you can see the whole man in perspective. He's had quite a year of it. Firstly, he had an appendicectomy and the wound became infected. He was made redundant from his fork-lift driving job. Then his girlfriend left him as money was tight, and just as he was picking himself up by doing some painting and decorating for a neighbour he fell off a ladder and fractured his radius. Unfortunately, the break is into the wrist joint.'

'That could cause complications when he tries to regain movement,' Jane added pensively.

She glanced past Dirk's shoulder to see a young man of about twenty-two who was sitting in the waiting area. He appeared to be nursing his right hand, cradling it on his lap. Tall and thin, he might have been strikingly handsome if it hadn't been for the dark circles under his eyes and the defeated look about him.

Just then Graham Walker and a few of the newly qualified physios trooped into the office.

Dirk greeted them all by name and took the opportunity to give an impromptu mini-lecture on the hand. As he slotted Harry's X-rays into the viewer he began, 'The break is at the lower end of the radius, and you can see that it's about a centimetre deep. Because Harry used to do quite a bit of labouring work, lifting packing boxes and the like, you can see that the bone in the hand is very strong. The trabeculae, or little beams of bone struts, are well marked.'

Then Dirk slotted the follow-up X-ray next to it. 'This was taken some weeks later. What can you see here?'

'Hmm. . .' Graham spoke up quickly. 'The bones are quite osteoporotic from the general viewpoint, although the fracture appears to have healed.'

'Exactly,' Dirk nodded. 'Another complication. Unfortunately a less experienced plaster-room nurse applied the cast too tightly. Harry had a lot of swelling and tingling, but fortunately rushed next door, where a neighbour used the dog's nail-clippers to cut the plaster and relieve the pressure.'

'Was there any nerve damage?' queried Jane.

'Fortunately not, thanks to the prompt use of the nail-clippers. Harry was rushed back to hospital and given a properly fitting cast. But that problem, together with the fact that he got the infection following surgery, has given him rather a negative view of medicine.'

Scanning his little class with a critical eye, Dirk asked, 'If the oedema or swelling hadn't been caught and treated straight away, what might have been the possible complications?'

Jane answered promptly, 'Fibrosis of the soft tissues could have occurred. And this could have led to a loss in suppleness, together with the flattening of the arches of the hand.'

'Good answer,' he nodded encouragingly, and she thought she caught the hint of a smile in those emerald eyes.

Dirk continued his lecture. 'The hand has so many small jonts that it can easily stiffen. Apart from the movements under the voluntary control of the patient, what are the involuntary ones—Jane again?'

She felt confident when she replied, 'Spin, glide and roll.'

'Excellent. I can see Harry will be fine with you.'

Jane felt quite elated by this unexpected praise, and she had to concentrate hard to listen on.

'But, apart from the physical effects, injury to the hand can have a psychological overlay. The hand is a highly evolved organ, and can be used in acts of great power as in a knock-out in boxing, or for extreme gentleness of touch—for example stroking a lover's cheek.'

God! I hope I'm not blushing now, thought Jane. Because when Dirk spoke with the softer side of his voice, and with obvious care and consideration for his patients, the old magnetism started to flow again, just as it had on *that* night under the stars.

He was talking again, and she returned after considerable effort.

'The word "hand" is used in everyday language. For example, handsome can be applied to a man, and a person's character is judged by the firmness or the limpness of his or her handshake.'

During this mini-lecture Jane frequently observed Harry Adamski by using her peripheral vision, and when there was a lull in the lecture she observed, 'Harry does seem to be in quite a bit of pain.'

'Yes,' nodded Dirk. 'That's a problem that must be your first priority, Jane. And, of course, perception of pain can be directly influenced by the patient. It's been neurologically known for some time that stimulating the mechanoreceptors, and putting diversional thoughts into the patient's mind, can directly diminish pain.'

'Yes,' said Graham, 'I've noticed it when my wife comforts my children after they've bumped and bruised themselves. When she says, "I'll rub and kiss it better," it really does work.'

The softness of Dirk's smile touched Jane's heart.

'Exactly,' he amplified. 'That age-old maxim is rooted in scientific fact.' He turned to her. 'That's one of the reasons I've brought Harry straight for physio—I'd like this pain cycle broken as soon as possible. And, as you all know, if it isn't treated soon and effectively then it may actually become "programmed" into the patient's mind.'

Jane knew the sense of all this. And she also knew the importance of Dirk's next words.

'And we shouldn't forget that pain is always real to the patient, whether it's pathological or has a psychological overlay.'

When the general talk was over, Dirk repacked the X-rays.

'Jane, I'd like Harry to start with a gentle first

treatment, and to include hot wax because his skin is so dry and scaly.'

'Has he just this minute been extricated from the plaster?' she asked.

'Yes. I've brought him straight here from the plaster-room.'

Jane knew she had to choose her next words with diplomacy. 'Immediately after the removal of a cast, wax baths are inadvisable, sir. The wax has been shown to cause a vasodilation of the capillaries, and at this very early stage it could lead to increased swelling.'

The situation could have been a bit difficult, because she had argued her point in front of her fellow physios. Fortunately Dirk seemed to take no offence, unlike other doctors who might feel insecure about their lack of knowledge.

'I didn't know that before,' he said. 'But it sounds physiologically correct. Fine, then, but what treatment do you recommend?'

'Soaking the hand in the whirlpool bath has proved very helpful, and I can regulate the water temperature easily.'

'Good, I'll remember that for future patients. Come and meet Harry now.'

Jane was surprised that Dirk had been so affable and accommodating. Obviously his charming mood was still in play. He perplexed her.

Harry Adamski looked pleased that Dirk had

taken the trouble to make the introduction to Jane himself.

Now Jane was examining Harry's hand on a pillow on a table in the hand rehabilitation area. 'You've got the long tapering fingers of an artist. Do you play an instrument?' she asked.

Breaking his transfixed gaze on his hand, he replied sombrely, 'No, nothing like that.'

She continued the questions as she gently palpated the texture of his skin and the tone of his muscles. 'You've told me you're right-handed, but I can see that you use your left uninjured hand as easily as if you were ambidextrous.'

He didn't look up this time. 'I suppose I must be. But then you get used to doing everything with your left hand when you can't use the other.'

'You'll be surprised how quickly we can make your injured hand more functional,' she interjected encouragingly.

She made her initial examination deliberately short, because she didn't want to pull Harry about too much. If she induced a lot of unnecessary pain at this stage, then he would lose all confidence in her and the proposed treatment.

'I think we'll try the whirlpool for a start. Then I'll put some hydrous ointment on to your skin, because it's dry, and then I'll cut you a

length of Tubigrip that'll make your hand feel
more comfortable.'

'Is that some sort of bandage?' he queried.

'Yes, it's like an elasticated tube of fine
material. It'll feel as if it's supporting your
tissues. As it's been encased in the plaster for
so many weeks, I expect your hand feels as if
some vital external support is now missing.'

'That's just it; my whole hand feels fragile,'
Harry agreed.

Jane escorted him to the whirlpool armbath
in the hydrotherapy section, and after this treatment she lightly massaged in the hydrous ointment. Then she measured up Harry's hand for
the correct size of Tubigrip and slipped it on.

'Now, although you'll come every day for
treatment, it's important that you do some exercises at home,' she told him. She fetched a Nerf
ball from the nearby cupboard and placed the
sponge ball, which was slightly larger than a
croquet ball, on the table before them. 'Can you
pick it up?'

He made a few attempts, but couldn't get a
firm grasp.

'All right, I can see that's a bit advanced at
the moment,' she interjected hastily, not wanting him to become too despondent. 'Place the
Nerf ball in your injured hand by using your
other hand. . .and now spread your fingers
around it.' She helped him to spread his fingers

wide and position his thumb in opposition.
'Now try and squeeze.'

'It's easier like this.' A glimmer of triumph
flickered through Harry's eyes. 'And because
the ball is made of foam it doesn't hurt at all.'

'Exactly,' Jane encouraged. 'When you're at
home, do that exercise ten times every hour
you're awake, and I'll see you at the same time
tomorrow.'

Over the next couple of days treating Harry
proved to be hard work. He did everything he
was told, but always remained detached and
within himself. She put this down to the fact that
he had no job to go back to.

But if Harry was hard going then Tom
Gulliver was just the opposite. He was a delight
to treat. Over his last few treatments Jane had
progressed him to lifting weights.

Now, in the progressive resisted exercise area
to one side of the big gym, Tom sat on a wooden
chair under the Westminster pulley system.

'I'm to work my biceps next,' he announced
eagerly.

'Well remembered,' praised Jane. 'Do you
remember how many lifts you did yesterday?'

'Yeah, fifty times with both arms.'

Uncle Chuck, who was standing to one side,
chuckled, 'He remembers every detail.'

Tom gripped the handles and began pulling
slowly and evenly. All the time he counted out
loud.

Jane had elected to make him do bilateral exercises because in this way he could be distracted from thinking that his right arm was the one that had been painful.

'Good lad,' beamed Uncle Chuck. 'That's ten more than yesterday.'

Jane handed Tom his PRE chart. 'Now write that in the appropriate column.'

Two days ago his ability to write in his recorded repetitions had been shaky, but today he seemed to have good control, even if his numbers were a bit large for the lines.

Tom worked determinedly on through several sets of muscles, then announced, 'And now I'll exercise my favourite muscle. . .serrat—serratus anterior.'

'It's amazing how quickly you've picked up the names of the muscles—especially as they're all in Latin,' Jane commended.

'Easy,' Tom grinned. 'Uncle Chuck said the serrated edge of his saw was like the bulk of my muscle on the side of my chest.'

The older man looked fit to burst with pride. 'Yes, the lad helped me saw some logs last night.'

'I'm highly impressed,' laughed Jane. 'It seems that Tom's rehab goes on at home as well. But,' she added, 'don't forget you've got to see Dr Blackwell here in the physio clinic at three o'clock tomorrow.'

'Don't worry about us,' Uncle Chuck interjected. 'We'll be here on time.'

When Tom had finished his treatment, the older man said, 'Here are the keys of the truck, Tom; wait for me while I have a word with Jane.'

The lad waved goodbye cheerfully, and when he was out of sight Uncle Chuck began, 'You've worked a positive miracle with him. He's brighter than at any time since his accident. And he seems to be learning so rapidly now.'

'It's the mental and physical stimulation,' Jane explained. 'But I believe your part has contributed significantly too.'

Uncle Chuck suddenly looked serious and he spoke slowly. 'The lad told me about that voodoo business the other night. Now he believes that it can't cross the water. Thank God! That was a brilliant way of dealing with him, because it dealt with his mind at his level.'

'Well, I'm glad it's worked out for the best.' Jane raised her eyebrows.

'Of course, he doesn't confide much. And I think if I'd been the first person he told, I'd have just got mad. I wouldn't have used the psychology that you did, and I might have made the situation worse.'

'Fate just put those words into my head,' she told him. 'It wasn't as if I consciously thought it out before I spoke.'

'Fate or whatever, the lad's better, and that's

all that counts. And I shall tell Dr Blackwell tomorrow. . . His mother's a bit tied up at the moment.'

Jane was sorry that Tom's mother wasn't going to put in an appearance. But she was so elated, she could have danced a jig on the spot! Now Dirk would have to eat his words of condemnation. Not only would he see that Tom was physically recovered, but good old Uncle Chuck was going to tell the story as it really happened.

Unusually, Boyd Harvey was on treatment that afternoon. He had overslept, and his aunt had rung with abject apologies and pleadings for another appointment.

His treatment was over, and now he was standing as tall as he could for his final measurement. The physical strain to stretch upwards showed on his face.

'Have I made the mark yet?' he asked anxiously.

'Still four millimetres short. Are you tilting your pelvis correctly?'

'Yes, yes, I'm doing everything exactly right.'

'It's a minuscule measurement,' sighed Jane. 'Perhaps we can gain it with more traction in future.'

'Do you think I'll make the mark by Thursday?'

'The day after tomorrow?' she almost croaked. 'But I thought you told me your assessment was next week?'

'No.' He shook his head vehemently.

Jane gulped. She had to get that four millimetres somehow.

'I'm relying on you Jane.' He sounded pathetic. 'When I'm in the police so many opportunities will open up for me. I'll be just like Dad, and I'll have money to buy a big house, a cabin by the lake, and holidays in Europe.'

Jane stared at him. Dirk's ominous words about this young man not being suitable for the police rang in her head.

'Yes, I've got it all worked out,' Boyd continued. 'I'll marry a police girl, because, as Dad says, that's the only sort of woman who'll understand what sort of pressures I'll be under. She'll have to be a great asset to my future career.'

He's programmed like a robot, she thought. Then, on a more critical level, Am I really doing the right thing by treating him? But then the police examination committee would weigh his qualities carefully and in the final analysis their professional judgement would decide.

She was still thinking about Boyd and the missing four millimetres when she bought up the topic with Graham in the Outpatients office.

'Pity he can't wear his shoes and put some hydraulic lifting mechanism inside,' he commented.

'That's no good,' Jane explained. 'He has to be barefoot for the measurement.'

'Ah, well, fate will decide.' Graham shrugged his shoulders.

'Why are you reading that old book about the foot?' Jane leaned over for a closer inspection.

'I'm going back to university in September to take my Master's. And I thought I'd write something about the foot for my thesis.' He yawned. 'But the idea of all that study makes me tired, so I think I'll give the reading a rest.'

As a bookmark he inserted a picture postcard of a bridge that was opening in its middle.

'A bridge that can be raised. . .a hydraulic mechanism. . .the foot. . .the arches of the foot. . . Yes! You've just given me a brilliant idea, Graham,' Jane told him. 'The internal lift for Boyd's missing four millimetres lies in the ability to raise the arches of his feet using his lumbrical muscles!'

'Aha! That's a neat piece of thinking, and such a sweet idea. You're on to a winner there, Jane.'

And Jane could hardly wait until the following morning when she tried her theory out.

'Brilliant!' cried Boyd as he made the magic four millimetres. 'Now I'm made for life.'

The day had got off to a wonderful start, and it would end just as successfully too, Jane thought, when Dirk Blackwell examined Tom in clinic. Then he'd have to admit that the cold hard facts of science weren't the only treatments that could be applied in modern medicine.

'Hello, Jane. Are you helping me in clinic this afternoon?'

She looked up suddenly from sorting the charts on the desk. Dirk's delight showed in the gleam of his eyes.

'Yes, Claire's gone to an unexpected management meeting,' she told him.

'I'm glad I've got company. Now, let's see who we've got on the list.'

The sleeve of his starched white coat brushed lightly past her arm. Although it was only the slightest of touches it sent a physical thrill through her.

'Tom Gulliver's set for three o'clock.' His eyes bored into hers. How quickly he changed. 'As you know, I didn't examine him for this shoulder problem, but I had a long talk with the junior doctor who did. He said the boy was extremely reluctant to be examined, and he was withdrawn and uncommunicative.'

Jane let him go on.

'However, he felt that the boy's problem might be due to a soft tissue injury of the capsule, as there was a typical pattern of restricted movement. And if that's the case I doubt we'll see much progress for weeks.'

'Oh, no,' Jane spoke up. 'Tom is completely better and uses his arm quite normally now.'

'In a week?' He raised one black eyebrow sceptically.

'With respect, the problem was psychosomatic——' she began.

He cut her off with the blackest of looks. 'Don't tell me you've got this hocus-pocus white magic still in your head after all I told you about fringe medicine? I trust you've treated this boy along proper scientific lines?'

'That's exactly what I have done, sir. And you'll see for yourself at three o'clock.' She quelled the surge of annoyance that she felt. Sometimes she burned to tell Dirk about her father's death, but not yet.

The first half of the clinic progressed smoothly. But as the time wound round to ten to three Tom's non-appearance made Jane feel apprehensive. For every treatment Uncle Chuck had always brought the boy at least ten minutes before the allotted time. She hoped nothing had happened to make them late.

Fortunately the clinic was running behind schedule, so at ten past three she took the opportunity to slip across to the main secretarial office and ring the Gulliver household. She let the number ring for what seemed like an eternity before she replaced the receiver. Dirk would be bound to make something of this if her patient didn't turn up, so she asked a secretary to keep trying.

Dirk was busy dictating notes on to his tape

recorder. There might still be time for Tom to turn up, so Jane went to organise the next patient.

'Mrs Louise Feeley!' she called as she scanned a row of waiting patients.

'*Ms* Feeley, darling.' A woman of about fifty who was dressed more like a teenager stood up.

'Come this way, please.' Jane indicated an empty examination-room.

Once inside, Ms Feeley gave an exaggerated sigh of relief. 'I'm so glad these are proper rooms, and that I'm not to be examined in a cubicle with flimsy curtains. . . You see, my problem is a little intimate.'

She had the look of a plump pussycat who was quite used to getting her own way, and she had a slight seductive purr to her voice.

'Could you get undressed so that Dr Blackwell can examine the part?' asked Jane politely.

Louise Feeley grinned mischievously. 'Unfortunately I don't think that'll be necessary—I only broke my jaw.'

'OK,' Jane laughed at her own mistake. 'Ah, here's Dr Blackwell now.'

'Hello, Louise. Now let's take a look at you,' Dirk began. 'You look one hundred per cent better than when I last saw you.'

'Thanks, Doctor,' she almost purred.

'Now, open your mouth wide. . .good, and now close. . .and move your jaw from side to side.'

Louise followed his instructions quite easily.

'That all looks very satisfactory. Any problems with eating?'

'None.'

'Then I think we've done all we can for you, Louise.' He stepped back.

'But there is just one problem. . .' She sounded slightly husky.

By this time Jane was intrigued. What could the intimate problem be?

'It's this dreadful loss of sensation around my lips,' she explained, lowering her eyelashes coyly.

'Umm. . .' Dirk stroked his chin. 'Does that cause a problem when you're drinking?'

'No. . .but it's having such a dreadful effect on my love life. The lack of sensation seriously hampers my enjoyment when kissing.'

Jane thought Dirk did well not to betray even a flicker of amusement, but he continued most professionally.

'Yes, I remember there was some damage to your inferior dental nerve. I'm afraid there's not a lot we can do about that, but the problem may well ease in time.'

'But sensation and touch are so important to a woman at *certain* times.'

'Umm. . .' Dirk nodded slowly. 'It's strange that you didn't complain of this problem at the time of the accident.'

Looking innocent, Louise answered, 'I didn't

have any opportunity to kiss anyone here in the hospital. Your doctors are all so stand-offish.'

Dirk laughed outright, and Jane hid a grin behind her hand. 'And quite rightly, Louise,' Dirk continued. 'It's called professional etiquette. But I can see there's no trouble with your muscles, because you're pouting very nicely now.'

'Poof! Now you're making fun of me, Dr Blackwell. It's just that my lawyer thought I ought to bring the matter up because my compensation case comes up before the board soon.'

'Nice try, Louise!' Severity tinged Dirk's tone. 'I'll write down what you say you feel in a letter to the board, but I can't promise anything.'

After Louise had left, he whispered close to Jane's ear, 'Good job I had you as my chaperon!'

They shared a good laugh about Louise. But by four o'clock Jane was quite agitated by Tom's absence. And she knew that Dirk had an appointment on the wards later.

As the last clinic patient left, she knew time had run out. Dirk screwed the top back on to his fountain pen and turned in his swivel chair to meet her square-on.

'What happened to Tom Gulliver?' he asked.

'I don't know, Dr Blackwell; he's always been on time for appointments before.'

Annoyingly he started to drum his fingertips on the desk. 'Perhaps you could use some of that white-coat magic that you so ardently believe in, Jane. How about, "Abracadabra", or "Hey presto"? Surely you'll be able to conjure your patient up that way?'

'Don't be so damned patronising!' she shot back. She could see his father's attitude in his whole bearing now. On a calmer note she added, 'If you could just wait a few more minutes I'm sure he'll be here.'

He sighed exaggeratedly and stood up slowly, stretching his arms above his head. 'Sorry, Jane, I'm needed on the wards. And without any clinical evidence I'll have to conclude that my colleague's judgement was correct.'

No! Jane cried inside. She was furious as he turned and walked through the door.

Suddenly Uncle Chuck hurried on to the scene. He was breathing heavily and was red in the face. 'Sorry, Dr Blackwell, but we had a flat tyre and the lad helped me change the thing. Good job too! It was damned hard work.'

CHAPTER FOUR

DIRK's face was a picture of astonishment as Tom rushed up moments after Uncle Chuck. And Jane was jubilant.

'Sorry I'm late,' Tom excused himself. 'But Uncle Chuck said I couldn't see a doctor with my hands all mucky like a grease-monkey.'

So much for the withdrawn, uncommunicative lad whom the junior doctor had examined only a week ago! I'm on to a winner here, thought Jane.

'I'm glad you've made it, because I've been thinking a lot about you lately.' Dirk opened the door to the cubicle and ushered everyone inside. Then, 'Slip off your T-shirt,' he ordered.

Tom sloughed off the garment with one easy lightning movement. And the puzzlement on the doctor's face deepened. Jane took the T-shirt and hung it over the back of the wooden chair.

Dirk motioned Tom to sit on a stool while he began palpating the shoulder girdle. 'It looks as if you've made a remarkably fast recovery since Dr Midwinter saw you in clinic last,' he remarked.

'Jane's made me work real hard, and I'm all

the better for it.' Tom's clear, smiling eyes looked up at the doctor.

And Jane was pleased to see that wherever Dirk probed, and however he stretched Tom's arm, the boy betrayed no sign of guarding or pain.

'Now, can you move both arms above your head?' Dirk demonstrated.

'Easy.' Tom followed the movements without hesitation. 'And I can lift my arms out to the side, and behind my back, and my neck.' He chattered on quickly, showing all the free range exercises that Jane had taught.

'Excellent.' Dirk looked impressed. 'But can you do this tricky movement? Can you put you left hand in the small of your back, and then put your right hand behind your back so that both hands touch at the back?'

He took up the position easily himself so that he could interlace his fingers.

'No sweat.'

'You're more flexible than I am,' laughed Dirk. 'You can get the palms of your hands together. But how about strength? Let me test you for that.' He went through all the major muscle groups, giving hard resistance so that Tom's muscles stood out with good definition.

Glancing at Jane, Dirk nodded in approval. And she couldn't help grinning back.

'That was easier than my weight training,' interjected Tom. 'I've lifted tons and tons of weights in the gym.' He began to recite the names of all the muscles, all the weights and the number of repititions.

'Hold on! Hold on!' laughed Dirk. 'I believe you. You're very enthusiastic about this. Have you got aspirations to go to the Olympics as a weight-lifter?'

Tom looked serious. 'No, but I'd like to make the position of pitcher in the school baseball team.'

'You've made an excellent recovery with Jane. But, Tom, how exactly did you injure your arm?'

The doctor's question had an immediate effect. Tom became withdrawn and hung his head, and began to chew his lower lip.

Obviously not wanting to see the lad suffer in any way, Uncle Chuck intervened.

'I'd appreciate it if I could have a private word with you, Dr Blackwell, on this subject. Would it be possible for Jane to take Tom to a wash-basin so that he can have a proper wash?'

Dirk caught the significance. 'Of course—go along, Tom. And Jane, see what you can do about getting that grease mark off his cheek. He looks as though he's half painted for an Indian war dance.'

Relief suddenly spread over Tom's face, and he grabbed his T-shirt and followed Jane.

'We'll be back in a few minutes,' she advised discreetly.

As she escorted Tom to a washbasin in the main treatment area, he started to give a description of how they had changed the tyre, and this continued all the way through the clean-up operation.

After a suitable time had elapsed, and Tom was spick and span, they walked back.

The look of frank admiration in Dirk's eyes told Jane that Uncle Chuck had put the record straight.

Shaking Tom's hand, Dirk said, 'You've done excellently. What would you say if we discharged you from physio now? Do you think you'd be all right?'

'Yeah, that's great! And I'll continue my exercises when I help Uncle Chuck saw the logs.' Tom turned his eyes slowly to Jane. 'Jane fixed me up, she got me going again.'

'I know all about that,' Dirk answered reassuringly. And when the older man and Tom left the clinic finally, the doctor turned to Jane and said, 'Congratulations. That was a job well done.'

Thrusting his fists deeply into his trouser pockets, he sighed and looked down. He seemed to study his well-polished black shoes for some time before looking up and meeting Jane's gaze.

'I owe you one hell of an apology,' he told her. 'I jumped to conclusions and bawled you out, without even giving you the courtesy of explaining the facts.'

His eyes were darkly troubled as he continued, 'It's true that I was tired that first time I condemned you in the outpatients office, and my judgement was clouded by the case of the diabetic man. But in reality those reasons are no excuse.'

'Don't blame yourself,' she interjected softly. 'I understood, and therefore it's easy to forgive.'

'You've a generous heart, Jane. I might have known that.'

He paused. 'And there was another reason why I behaved so aggressively and like a bastard to you. . .'

Her heart quickened. She knew he was about to refer to their relationship on a more personal level.

'I've never been able to forget our experience at the Old-Timers' Cabin. Although fleeting, that time was very special to me, so when you stood up to me and tried to argue your points about Tom's treatment I could only see red. You seemed so very different from the wonderful woman I'd known.'

Jane's mind melted at his declaration, and she knew it was a big man who could apologise, especially like this.

'And your psychology with Tom was outstanding,' Dirk added. 'Even here in clinic just now, it was obvious that the situation still caused him some deep fear. And he didn't want to discuss it. As doctors, we all try and get through to our patients, but in this case we failed. How did you do it?'

'I think you're being too harsh with yourself,' said Jane. 'In Physio the whole atmosphere and the relationship with patients is much more relaxed.' She raised her eyebrows and continued, 'With Tom, I think it was just luck. He was at the stage when he needed to spill out the whole voodoo incident. And again I was just lucky when I thought of the right thing to say.'

'Now, I don't believe it was wholly luck. You diverted the boy's mind in an extremely clever way, then you built on that with some positive dynamic rehab.'

This unexpected praise from Dirk made Jane blush, and this deepened even more when he took her hand.

'I'm glad it was you who treated Tom, and I'm even more pleased that we've met up again like this.' The warmth of his large hand seemed to infuse itself into her bloodstream. And when she looked up into his dilated eyes she could feel the emotion of that starlit night again.

'I'm already late for the wards,' he added, 'and I'm a bit tied up for the next few days, but I'd like us to get together again.'

'I'll look forward to that.' Her hasty heart put the words into her mouth.

Swiftly he bent to kiss her fingertips. 'Until then,' he murmured, and left.

Jane was ecstatic that the running argument had been settled so well. She had been wrong about Dirk—he was nothing like Dr Blackwell the cardiologist. Here was a man who could weigh up the situation and admit that he had been wrong. And she was thrilled at the idea of meeting him again. After all, her father had told her to let the past go, and that was exactly what she would do.

When Boyd made his entrance into Physio for his final treatment before his medical examination for the police, the whole department knew all about it.

Jane heard his loud, clear-cut instructions before she even saw him.

'Wheel me through the gym to the traction area. Turn right here. . .no, right!'

As she rounded a corner she saw her patient lying on a stretcher, and being pushed by two ambulancemen from a private company.

'I see you've arrived on time with your entourage,' Jane quipped.

'Yep. This is my big day,' he laughed back.

'Can't say that we've ever transported a patient like this one——' One of the ambulancemen shook his head.

'Aw, you don't mind,' Boyd interrupted. 'It's

all business to you.' Looking up at Jane, he added, 'My aunt sorted all this out.'

Once in the treatment area, he scooted agilely on to the traction table. 'OK, men, you can take a rest for forty minutes, but make sure you're back here on time, because I can't be late.'

They laughed and walked off, shaking their heads.

'You're very confident about passing, Boyd. But haven't you got other written parts in this exam?' Jane threaded the straps through the thoracic buckles of the harness and pulled them tight.

'That'll be plain sailing. Dad's made me practise with heaps of old entry papers.' He yawned. 'I think I could even do them in my sleep now.'

'Well, just as long as you don't take that cocksure attitude with you when you're patrolling the streets. The world can be a dangerous place out there.'

'I'll be fine. Anyway, I won't stay in the lower ranks for long. I'll take more exams and work my way right to the top. That's the place to be.'

She found his driving ambition a little frightening, but perhaps such a job would demand it.

When the treatment was over and he was back on the stretcher he grasped Jane's hand and shook it hard. 'This is going to be the best day of my life, and it's thanks to you. I won't forget.'

'Let me know of your success as soon as you can,' she said.

'Of course, I'll come back straight away and bring you the biggest box of chocolates you've ever seen. You've certainly been worth that much to me.'

He looked on top of the world as the ambulancemen pushed him through the department doors. But later, as Jane erased his name from the timetable board, she felt a strange cold shiver run up her spine. Shaking it off, she put it down to the fact that some of the cold cleaning fluid was running down her wrist.

Harry Adamski's hand had improved slightly since he had been on the whirlpool treatment, but his depressed attitude had not.

'The swelling has completely gone now, Harry. I think we can progress to the wax baths today,' Jane told him.

'I suppose that's something,' he replied dully.

By the edge of the large wax bath, Jane gave a demonstration. 'This is the way it's done,' she explained. 'Dip your whole hand in so that the wax comes up at least six inches above your wrist. Then, as you can see on my little finger, the shine becomes dull after a moment or two. That's the time when you can dip your hand again and build up another coat. If you do this six times you'll have a thick covering that'll keep in the heat for about twenty minutes.'

Gingerly he dipped his hand, then brought it out quickly. 'It's hotter than the whirlpool!' he exclaimed.

'Yes, but it won't burn you. Look. . .' She peeled the wax from her own finger. 'It just feels that hot because you're not used to it.'

Gently she pushed his hand into the wax, and then guided him out.

'Yes, you're right, it's OK,' Harry agreed.

He repeated the procedure, then Jane wrapped his hand in plastic and covered it with thick, specially made blanket material.

'Don't move your fingers, otherwise it'll break the seal and the heat will escape,' she advised. She positioned his hand on a pillow on the table, then left him reading a daily newspaper.

It was a pity that there weren't any other hand patients on treatment at the same time, because group work was always effective in raising morale.

Suddenly the intercom summoned Jane to the general office, where Alice the secretary told her about a new patient.

'Her name is Sister Veronica, and she's from the Convent of the Holy Cross. Apparently she's just come to Canada from England, and she was wondering if she could have treatment as soon as possible as she came out of plaster in England and hasn't had any active physio since.'

'A nun. . .' mused Jane. 'I was just hoping for another hand patient. Yes, I'll take her straight away. Thanks.'

She took the requisition and found the nun sitting in the waiting area.

'I'm Jane Easter, and I'll be the physio looking after you, Sister Veronica,' she said.

She was astounded by her new patient's classical beauty. She was in her early twenties, just like Jane, and she could have been one of Raphael's Madonnas.

'Good morning, Jane. I didn't expect someone to see me so quickly. Glory be! I've never known such efficiency.'

Jane couldn't help grinning. 'We try our best, Sister. Now, if you'd like to come this way.

'I've got company for you, Harry,' Jane explained as she made the introductions between the two patients.

'I'm very pleased to meet you.' Sister Veronica shook Harry's uninjured hand quite naturally, and smiled radiantly.

The effect on the young man was instant. He sat up straighter, and his eyes brightened. But he could only manage a mumbled self-conscious, 'Hi.' Then he went back to reading his newspaper.

Jane made Sister Veronica comfortable at the big table by placing a pillow under her hand, then she withdrew a notepad and pen from her tunic pocket.

'I see from your requisition that you've had a Colles' fracture of your right wrist. That's one of the most common we see here in Physio.'

'That's exactly what my doctors in England told me. But I only broke it across the lower end of the radius, about an inch above my wrist.'

Jane nodded and scribbed notes. 'How exactly did you injure it?' she asked.

'Like all accidents, it was rather silly,' confessed the nun. 'I was doing a little dusting, and I stepped back off a chair to avoid a spider. Then I fell, and landed on my outstretched hand.'

This was a typical mechanism of injury, Jane knew.

Sister Veronica continued, 'I was in the plaster for a month, and I've been out for four days now.'

Surveying the nun's hand, Jane said, 'It looks in very good condition. Have you been using it?'

'Oh, yes, I've done everything my English physio told me; shoulder and elbow exercises. And after the plaster was removed I was told to soak my hand in warm water twice a day and massage in some baby lotion.'

'Excellent.' Jane palpated the hand. 'There's no evidence of swelling at all, and the skin looks in remarkable condition.'

She checked the movements and then the

strength of all the muscles, and jotted down her findings.

It amused Jane to see Harry surreptitiously glancing at Sister Veronica, then raking his fingers through his hair so that it was sleeked down to his head. He's smitten with her, Jane smiled to herself. Not that he was likely to get very far—after all, she had taken a vow of chastity. But, from the rehabilitation point of view, she was convinced that he would now do his exercises with great enthusiasm.

As there was no swelling in the hand, Jane decided to give the nun the wax bath treatment. And by the time it was applied, and she was comfortably relaxing at the table, it was time to start Harry's active exercises.

'Peel the wax off yourself,' Jane instructed, 'then wipe your hand in the terry towel.'

'It's made my hand sweat a bit, but it feels very good.' He sounded more positive than ever before.

Turning to the nun, Jane said, 'Watch these exercises now, because you'll be doing them later.'

Harry followed Jane's instructions enthusiastically, manipulating the wax and making the pancake, then a sphere, then a sausage, and then a weird shape that he insisted was a racing car.

'Now, roll it into a sphere once more,' Jane continued.

'No, a white billiard ball,' he teased. He held it lightly and with improved precision.

'More like the moon at night,' interjected Sister Veronica.

'Just as you like,' he smiled softly.

'The full moon last night was absolutely gorgeous,' the nun continued. 'It always amazes me how it looks two or three times bigger when it's on the horizon than when it's high in the heavens.'

Jane was surprised that Harry had quite a lot to say on this subject, and as he looked so animated she didn't insist that he get on with his work.

'That apparent growth in size is a real phenomenon,' he explained. 'It's the same for the setting as for the rising moon on the horizon.' As he continued his eyes lit up. 'Many scholars have tried to explain the difference, but no one has proved a satisfactory theory to date.'

He was speaking with such authority that it made Jane intensely curious.

'Some believe that when the moon is high in the sky we're looking at it through a more rarefied atmosphere, and therefore it looks smaller. And then others say that when the moon is on the horizon, against a backdrop of trees and buildings, it looks bigger because the brain interprets it that way, as if it were sitting on the planet Earth.' He shook his head again and grinned. 'But it's just a brilliant illusion that can never be explained away.'

'Like magic.' Siser Veronica sounded captivated. 'A celestial magic.'

'Exactly,' he agreed. 'And magic can bring so much happiness into people's lives.'

And a little romantic magic is going to do your rehab the power of good, thought Jane. Fate, or something that couldn't be explained away by reason alone, had brought this nun to her small hand class.

'Oh, damn! I'd forgotten I was on call tonight.' Graham flopped down on a chair next to Jane. It was lunchtime and everyone had congregated in the staffroom.

'What's the problem?' Jane enquired.

'It's my son's birthday and as a treat I'd organised a party at McDonald's, and then we were going on to a movie. It was stupid of me to forget. And typically there are several chesty post-operative cases on the wards. I suppose I'll have to ring my wife and tell her to expect me when she sees me.'

'No, don't do that,' said Jane. 'I'll swap with you.'

'Great! You're an angel, Jane. I won't forget this.'

At the end of the day, when she had finished her work in Outpatients, Jane elected to stay at the hospital and have supper in the canteen.

The evening work proved to be hectic. As soon as she walked on to a ward the charge nurse would rush up with an urgent requisition for another patient. And so it was that she was kept busy until dusk.

Only when she felt assured that all the chesty patients were settled for the night did she set off for home. She walked quickly up the main avenue leading from the hospital. The road was noisy, as many people were spilling out on to the streets from the nearby restaurants.

Preparing to cross the road, she didn't hear the man's voice at first. Then she was startled and apprehensive.

CHAPTER FIVE

'JANE!' The man ran up to her, clutching a flat cardboard box. 'I didn't think you'd heard me the first time I called.'

She swung round, and was confronted with Dirk. His eyes sparkled brilliantly under the street-lights.

'You shouldn't be out on the streets all by yourself late at night,' he scolded.

'I've been on call at the hospital, and I've had rather a heavy night with some post-op chests,' she explained.

'Then how about relaxing with me? I've got a delicious Hawaiian pizza here. It's topped with bacon and pineapple pieces, and I'm sure I can find a bottle of white wine in the fridge.' His voice was so inviting. 'I'm starving.'

'Yes, I'd love to come,' she said. Her father had warned her that any thought of revenge would only cause her more pain. It was right to forget the past.

'I live in Newton Plaza.' He pointed to a tall modern apartment building. 'There's a short-cut down this back alley.' As he slid his arm around her shoulder, she was glad of his protective presence in the descending darkness.

The foyer of the Plaza was impressive with its plush red carpets that Jane's feet sank into.

'You're riding all the way to the penthouse with me tonight,' he grinned as he selected the lift button.

She felt that sinking feeling in the pit of her stomach as they gathered speed and ascended. But she wasn't quite sure if it was entirely due to the lift or the dark, handsome doctor.

Once inside the apartment, she exclaimed, 'It's brilliant up here! From this huge picture window in your sitting-room you must be able to watch glorious sunsets.'

'That's what I like about this bird-high place, and the sky is better than any framed picture because it's always changing.'

She turned and caught the laughter in his eyes.

The moon was slowly sinking on to the horizon, so they decided to eat in the kitchen, where the view was even more spectacular. They passed the time pleasantly talking, mostly about patients. And watching the moon reminded Jane of her little hand class.

'I think Harry Adamski is going to progress in leaps and bounds from now on,' she told him.

'Oh. . .have you been on a course and learnt some new treatment?'

She explained about Sister Veronica and how

the young nun's beauty had had a startling effect on the young man.

'Aha,' chuckled Dirk. 'What a pity she's taken her vows—she's hardly likely to break them or any of her habits for a *layman*.'

'That's slightly irreverent,' Jane laughed. 'And it's a terrible old joke anyway.' By now she was feeling very relaxed due to the effect of the wine and the delicious food.

'Old jokes are often the best,' he quipped back. Then, as he was sprinkling salt on to his last slice of pizza, he spilled a few grains on to the table.

'That's bad luck, Dirk. Pick a couple of grains up and throw them over your left shoulder.'

He looked at her with an expression of amusement and incomprehension. 'Don't tell me you're superstitious, Jane. I can't believe that—not after all the science training you've had.'

'Science is all well and good, but I don't believe in flying in the face of ill-luck. Just throw a couple of grains,' she insisted.

'I'll do no such thing. If I started scattering salt all over the floor, I'll only have to clean it up in two places.'

His stubbornness piqued her, so she went on boldly, 'Science can't explain away everything, surely. There are lots of examples in life. Haven't you ever suddenly thought about an old friend that you hadn't heard of or thought of for ages, and then out of the blue a letter or a telephone call comes from them?'

'No, I certainly haven't. And anyway, that sort of thing is purely coincidence.' He sipped his wine slowly. 'Next you'll be telling me you believe in extra-sensory perception.'

'I certainly don't disbelieve it. What about twins who've been born from the same egg? In my class at high school we had just such a pair. One day they both landed up with sprained ankles, and that was when one fell off a horse and the other was out riding her bike miles away.'

Dirk set down his glass deliberately, leaned back in his chair and looked at her sceptically. 'But that's no scientific basis for anything. Anyway, superstitions can lead to people being duped and other much more serious consequences. Magicians use illusions in their theatre shows—they do it for entertainment. But then there are some spirit mediums who use the illusions unscrupulously, and con some poor bereaved people out of a lot of money.'

'I agree with you there.' Dirk's sombre example made Jane think of her father, and there had been times when she desperately would have liked to talk to him.

Dirk went on, 'Look at that Tom Gulliver incident. That could have had bad consequences if you hadn't handled it properly, Jane. You used psychology, and that's a science.

Goodness knows what would have gone on in that poor boy's head otherwise.'

'But can't you accept that there are some things in heaven and earth that can't be explained by science alone?'

It seemed important to her now that Dirk's mind should have at least one open channel. She didn't want him to be as inflexible as his father.

'I'm a science man through and through. Everything has a logical explanation.'

'Not *quite* everything,' she said, turning to look through the window at the night sky. 'Look at the moon on the horizon. That's an illusion. It's at least three times bigger than when it's high in the sky, and no one can explain away that. Scientists have tried, but no one has come up with an ultimate solution.'

'Well, Jane, I can prove that's an illusion, and right here and now.' Dirk stood up and guided her towards the window where the view was better. 'First of all, the difference in size doesn't show up on photographs, and people who have lost one eye don't appear to see the illusion.'

'I don't believe you can magic this horizon moon and make it smaller.' Irritation crept into her voice.

'That's exactly what I will demonsrate. If you lie down on your back with your head towards the moon, and with your head hanging over the kitchen table, then you'd see the moon revert to its expected smaller size.'

She burst out laughing. 'You don't really expect me to lie on your kitchen table to try out this theory? I'm not at all sure your intentions are honourable.'

'You don't have to lie down; you can also stoop over and view this horizon between your legs.'

Jane shook her head and covered her eyes. 'This is completely crazy, absolutely crackpot.' She watched incredulously as he stooped over.

'Yes, it always works,' he answered. 'Come and stand by me, and see for yourself.'

She hesitated, then with grave reservations took up the ungainly position. 'Oh!' she exclaimed with a falling inflexion as the moon apeared to shrink. She stood up quickly and looked at it again. From her upright position it was large. And then again she stooped over. True enough, it looked small again.

Dirk shrugged his shoulders. 'So you can see for yourself, the perceived size of the moon depends on some physiological viewing mechanism involved with the eyes. I can't remember exactly what it is. . .but it truly is an illusion.'

'You've just explained away a beautiful piece of magic,' she accused.

'It's true that I've given the scientific rationale behind the illusion, but the moon is still there

in the sky, and lovers and everyone else on this
earth can still enjoy it.'

Damn it! she thought. His cool, scientific
mind could turn anything round. Flashbacks of
the arguments with his father began to invade
her mind. And it became imperative that she
find an example that he couldn't argue against.

With emotion past the simmering stage, she
began, 'What about people who literally die of
a broken heart? Some couples are so much in
love that when one dies the other dies too.
Surely that has a psychic origin?'

'The word broken isn't that misleading. We
know for a fact that fragmentation of the heart
muscle does happen in the course of myocardial
infarction. Following an intense emotion,
people can get a reflex spasm of the coronary
arteries, and if this is prolonged then degenera-
tion of the tissues can occur. So it's quite logical
that death from myocardial infarction in these
tragic cases is actually related to cause and
effect.'

'Dear God! I might have known you could
rationalise that away.' By now Jane was
intensely upset. She could feel herself becoming
hotter, and her face began to glow. Pin-pricks
of tears began to form in her eyes.

Dirk looked at her strangely. 'When I fall in
love with a woman, I hope it will be deeply and
irrevocably,' he said. 'If I'm lucky she'll feel the
same way about me. . .and then, however long

we had together, if she did die before me then I think I might die of that sort of broken heart.'

Jane gasped and the breath caught in her throat. Tears were threatening to spill as she looked at him. The intensity in his face was almost unbearable, and now she knew that *she* was the woman he referred to.

He came towards her, caught her in his arms, and held her close to his heart. 'Why are we arguing like this, Jane?' He stroked her hair, his fingers running down the nape of her neck. 'Sometimes you can be so stubborn. I can't imagine that our argument tonight stemmed solely from the spilling of a few grains of salt.'

She felt like telling him, revealing everything then and there. But something held her back.

'Tell me, tell me,' he urged softly.

His arms were tight about her, the warmth of his body such a comfort.

'Because—because. . .' She could feel the heat rising in her cheeks, and the tears about to cascade. Not since talking to her father had she spoken of the subject to a soul. Now was the time.

With great difficulty she fixed her gaze on Dirk's face. After a couple of steadying breaths, she began as coolly as possible, 'Your father is an eminent cardiologist, isn't he?' She named the hospital.

'Yes, he worked there for a couple of years until a few months ago. But what of it?'

Jane focused hard through tearful eyes. 'Because I believe your father was in some way responsible for the death of *my* father,' she said bluntly.

Dirk looked as though he had been forcibly hit about the face, the impact was so great. Then his emerald eyes narrowed to slits.

'What gives you the right to make such a slanderous accusation?' He bit the words out.

Jane was afraid. However, she stood her ground. But as Dirk's expression hardened she was lost for the right words.

'What right? Negligence, malpractice, or incompetence?' he demanded.

Now she felt her nerve waver. 'None of those exactly.'

'What, then?'

'Your father wouldn't listen. . .' She explained the situation briefly. 'I just had a terrible feeling of foreboding. . .like a premonition.' There, it was out. 'I've had them before, and they've been proved.'

He was inches in front of her within a split second, his fingers gripping hard into the flesh of her arms. 'Do you mean to tell me that my father's been judged by your damned mumbo-jumbo?' He didn't wait for her choked reply. 'Listen to me, you silly slip of a girl. My father is an expert, and the most caring, conscientious cardiologist in the world. I'm damned sure your father got all the available tests and treatment.'

'Yes—yes, he did.' She could feel the tears falling now. 'But there's always the unknown. . . If only he'd listened——'

'You pestered him, more likely, and he, being a good doctor, reassured you until he was blue in the face.'

'You're exactly like him when you're like this,' she spat back. 'Your arrogance is insufferable. You don't look like him facially, but your expression tells me everything.'

He let her go roughly, and stepped back, eyeing her coldly. 'You're right; I look like my mother. . . She died when I was thirteen. Dad brought me up single-handed, and if I look like him in any way then I'm damned proud.'

After a tense moment's silence he added, 'Who else have you told this fantasy to?'

'No one. My mother is still bereft; I wouldn't hurt her any more.'

The news that Dirk had been motherless at such a critical age took some seconds to sink in through Jane's heaving emotions. For an instant she saw his situation, and she felt a rise of empathy towards him. But she had no time to explore her feelings, because her bleeper sounded.

Startled and anxious, she looked down, brushing the tears from her eyes. 'I'd forgotten I was on call. . .'

'Go to the hospital,' Dirk ordered nastily. 'Do your ministering works, but if I ever catch you slandering my father to anyone I'll have you in court in double-quick time.'

She looked up quickly and caught the curl of his lip. He was hurt too.

Turning his back on her, he said, 'Get out of my apartment, Jane.' His words were ice-cold and cutting.

She fled, but she couldn't forget, not even after many days and many convoluted issues with patients.

One afternoon while Sister Veronica and Harry were on their wax treatments, Jane prepared for their upcoming exercises.

On the big hand table she placed an assortment of objects, coins, paper-clips, parts of a jigsaw, and several different thicknesses of ropes that could be tied into knots.

Surreptitiously Harry picked up one of the large foreign coins that was the size of a silver dollar, and concealed it in his uninjured left hand.

'Wasn't there a big coin on this table a moment ago?' he asked innocently.

'Yes. I didn't hear it drop on the floor.' Jane bent over to look.

'Ah, here it is. . . Just behind your ear, Jane!' exclaimed Harry.

The two women laughed, and Sister Veronica looked puzzled. 'How did you do that? I was watching you all the time.'

'I don't know. . .'. Harry still appeared innocent. 'The coin must have vanished into thin
air.' Then, a moment later, 'Ah, here it is again,
Sister—it was hiding behind the silver cross on
your habit.'

'Where did you learn that trick, Harry?' Jane
asked.

'Prestidigitation or sleight of hand can always
be fun,' he chuckled. 'It's my hobby—I've
wanted to be a magician ever since I was a little
kid. But I'm not that good.'

'I do so admire card tricks and this sort
of impromptu conjuring,' Sister Veronica
enthused.

Jane seized the opportunity to be positive. 'If
you practise with your exercises long enough,
Harry, I don't see why you shouldn't be as
supple and as dexterous with your right hand
as you are with your left.'

'That's exactly what I aim to do now,' he said
proudly.

Sister Veronica continued animatedly, 'I
remember my old grandmother once saw
Houdini on the stage. She said he was in a
strait-jacket, then he started to wriggle and
wriggle, and suddenly he was out of it!'

'Ah, now you're talking of my hero, and a
real master magician.' Harry leaned forward as
he could see he had intrigued the two women.
'Houdini wrote in his notes that if you could
dislocate your shoulder joints you could get out

superbly; he could never become panicky, as in the burial trick, otherwise he knew he'd fail.'

Jane was still thinking of Dirk surrounded by a black void, but then she heard the doctor's voice as he was walking through the department. Another cold chill numbed her. She hoped he hadn't heard any of this conversation—no doubt it would give him more fuel against her beliefs. And yet part of her ached for him, while other feelings caused her excruciating pain. Was this love? If it was, it wasn't fair or just.

With great difficulty Jane focused her mind on her patients. Both progressed well. Harry was able to thread paper-clips, and Sister Veronica was able to turn over playing cards.

Some aspects of Jane's job took her out of herself and her thoughts about Dirk. And one such brightness was Tom Gulliver.

'Here she is!' Tom called out excitedly as he ran up to Jane. He was followed closely by Uncle Chuck.

It was near the end of the afternoon and Jane was stacking away weights in the PRE area. 'Hello, you two,' she smiled. 'What are you doing back here?'

'I've got a present for you. It's for helping to fix me up,' Tom grinned broadly, and thrust a small package into her hands.

'That's very kind of you,' she answered, feeling the strange shape curiously.

'Open it up and see what you think!' Tom's excitement was infectious.

'Oh, it's a little black totem pole! Thank you, Tom.' She gazed at the carving. It was so strange and weird with its large, staring eyes of powerful animals. And there was a compelling force about it.

'You do like it, don't you?' Tom raced on. 'I chose it especially, because Uncle Chuck said the designs were supposed to be protective, and sometimes curative.'

She looked up into the young man's bright face. 'It's brilliant. I don't think I've ever had such a nice present from a patient.'

'I'm quite fit now, thanks to you,' he told her. 'And I want to chop down a big tree and carve a totem pole just like that one day. The real ones are thirty feet high and made from cedarwood.'

Uncle Chuck added, 'The lad likes the animals and the meanings behind the carving. North American Indians believe it's a magical art inspired by dreams and visions.'

'I'll give it pride of place in my living-room on the bookshelf,' Jane told them. 'And when I look at it, I'll think of you as a forestry man, Tom.'

The little present, though inexpensive, meant a great deal to Jane. And something touched her heart when Tom and Uncle Chuck left, because she overheard the lad say, 'I'll work real hard on the chores to pay you back.'

She was still examining the little carving when Dirk strode up. Every muscle in her body froze.

'Hello, Jane. What have you got there that's so fascinating?' The tone of his voice was so softly compelling. . .and there was another aspect. It touched the depths of her soul. She heard tenderness. Deep down did he regret their last quarrel?

Butterflies raced through her stomach. She felt sure he had come to instigate some sort of truce.

'Hello,' she mumbled, hardly daring to look straight up into his eyes. 'Look—Tom Gulliver gave me a totem pole as a present.' She forced a smile and handed it over for him to see. She would follow his lead.

He held the object lightly in his powerful hands. 'Hmm. . .the carving is very schematic, almost like that of Ancient Egypt.'

There was a silence. To Jane it was as deep as the break in her heart. Even though their acquaintance had been so short and turbulent, she knew a part of her soul desired Dirk, but in loving this man she felt as if she was being somehow disloyal to her father's spirit.

'I like the carving,' she said simply. But her emotions rose and unthinkingly she raced on, 'Apparently it's inspired by dreams, visions and the imagination. Tom wanted me to have it, because it's supposed to be magical and protective. I thought that was very sweet of him. And the idea of these legendary, supernatural figures appeals to me.'

Immediately she could have bitten her tongue. Why had she goaded Dirk?

His face became clouded, and she could see him battle for control. 'I don't like the way you see supernatural elements in everything, Jane.' He placed the little object on a nearby weight-lifting table. 'These ideas of yours cause me grave concern. It's only a small step from your way of thinking to more dangerous beliefs, like the occult, and *other* problems.'

She glared at him. 'I'm not that stupid about the occult. But I do believe there are forces that can't be explained by reason alone.'

'There you go again,' he rasped. 'Why can't you drop these stupid notions?' A muscle in his jaw twitched.

She looked at him steadily as she tried to control her breathing and block out the past. She knew they were really back on the argument of her father's death.

'How can you begrudge me the pleasure of this little object stemmed in legends?' And then when she saw the true concern in his eyes she remembered other things. 'The first night we met, your talk was all of myths and mysteries surrounding gems.' Her mind and emotions were whirling. Everything was so confusing.

'That was quite different, and those weren't my personal beliefs. They were only stories that my grandfather told me, and I told you purely for entertainment, and because they seemed to perfectly fit the mood of that evening.'

The very idea that they were purely chat-up lines made Jane see red. That evening had seemed so magical to her, and now he was explaining it away.

'If I remember rightly, Dirk, your first words were that we were "*fated* to dance. . .*at least*",' she pointed out.

He raised his black eyebrows. 'Did I say that? I can't remember. And anyway, I don't believe in fate. We forge our own destinies, Jane. We have the power to come to terms with the past, and to move on in life.'

She knew this was a direct reference to her father, but she chose to ignore it. 'So all your words that night were empty and without meaning,' she flared, her blue eyes darkening. Sometimes her sensual feelings for him were so strong. 'You're strait-jacketed in your science!' she accused. 'Why can't you broaden and open your mind? That would make you a more understanding doctor, and one who'd listen to patients and relatives and their points of view.' The true argument was out again!

It was as well that this part of the department

was deserted. Dirk's voice was low, but it carried a powerful warning.

'Listen, Jane—the other night when you accused my father I could have struck you, I was so livid. But. . .on reflection. . .I can understand *some* of your feelings.'

She looked away. The past was so painful. She didn't want it brought up again, and certainly not here at work. But Dirk pursued his points.

'You've obviously bottled all this bitter resentment up for a long, long time, and it's probably precisely because you haven't come to terms with it that you harbour this. . .this grudge.'

'It's no grudge,' she defended hotly.

'Listen, this problem is festering in you, causing great damage. Let me take you out tonight, so that we can discuss the whole thing. You'll feel better then. I'm sure you can come to terms with your father's death. . .but only if you let me help.'

Jane's emotions were reeling. She was afraid to face up to the situation. She panicked.

'I couldn't accept your help. . .certainly not on this matter. . .not if you were the last man on earth,' she flared.

His hand shot out and grabbed her elbow as she attempted to rush past him. 'Can't you see that I'm the only man who can help?' he demanded.

She looked up into his face, now grim but

clouded with concern. He cared for her—it was written in his expression and his voice. And, oh, how she longed to be free of the burden of the past.

But out of the corner of her eye she saw Claire Jousserand walking their way. Then the new director called to Dirk.

'Ah, Dr Blackwell! You're just the man I'm looking for.'

Taking the opportunity, Jane pocketed her totem pole. 'Excuse me, but I've some notes to finish.'

The moment had been interrupted and was now lost. She felt her whole body shaking. One part of her wanted to talk to Dirk, but another part held her back. Love and hate were inextricably intertwined in this matter. She thought it emotionally safer to give Dirk a wide berth in future.

CHAPTER SIX

'Excuse me, ma'am, I didn't mean to knock into you.'

It was Saturday, just after lunch, and Jane was walking to the supermarket to buy a carton of milk.

Admittedly she was deep in thought, so she hadn't seen the man coming out of the electrical store. Her mind seemed to turn constantly on Dirk these days, and their last argument burned in her still.

Now the shock of seeing those well-known emerald eyes made her step back.

Immediately Dirk's arms reached out to steady her. 'You look all in, Jane—you've got deep shadows under your eyes. I should say you've had a few sleepless nights.'

He was right, of course. 'It's hardly surprising in the circumstances.' She tried to sound aloof.

'I think you need a good prescription for relaxation. You're new to this province, and I bet you haven't visited the mountains yet. How would you like tea in the Rockies? It'll just be sightseeing, no heavy conversation.'

Slowly she raised her eyes, and his magic of

the night at the Old-Timers' Cabin went straight to her heart. She was torn with indecision.

'Purely rest and relaxation.' His voice was persuasive.

In the back of her mind she knew that the old problem of her father's death should be resolved. Perhaps, given time, Dirk could be that bridge to healing. In time. . .

'Yes, I'd love to come,' she answered quietly.

'Good girl,' he said reassuringly, and, pulling her arm through his, led her back to the Plaza.

In the kitchen he found a cooler, then started to fill it with soft drinks and food from the fridge. 'And I think we'll need a couple of loaves of bread too.'

'So much bread! How many sandwiches do you think we're going to eat?'

'It's not all for us.' He glanced at her. 'There are some mountain sheep who are very partial to this type of wholemeal.'

After the jeep had been satisfactorily packed, they headed for the highway. Soon they had left the city far behind, and the road stretched straight ahead like a great slash of grey towards the horizon. On either side, in the summer fields, Jane saw the hay lying in huge bundles. And the heat of the afternoon sun shimmered off the earth.

After some time Dirk broke the silence. 'I've been in the department several times lately, and heard some of the animated conversations in your hand class. It certainly sounds very entertaining.'

She chuckled. He made her feel relaxed. She felt there was no confrontation here. 'Ah, you mean Harry's stories about the great Houdini. Yes, I'm grateful to that magician, because I'm sure his example has inspired Harry, and I don't think I'll have any problems progressing him to weight-bearing exercises in the gym.'

Dirk nodded. 'I didn't hear the whole of the story, but how did Houdini escape from under an iced river?'

'Oh, that was very dramatic. And Houdini only managed to escape because of his remarkable lung capacity. Apparently he used to submerge himself in the bath and practise slow deep-breathing exercises. Harry says he could remain submerged for four minutes sixteen seconds.'

'Hmm. . .' Dirk sounded impressed. 'I can swim underwater for a couple of lengths, but I'm sure I couldn't stay under that long.'

Jane continued, 'On this occasion, Houdini was manacled and chained, and he dived off a bridge through a small hole in the ice into a river. To the great consternation of the crowd, he didn't appear for eight minutes. Apparently he unchained himself on the river bed in less than a minute, but when he rose to the surface the current had taken him downstream. He swam about underwater trying to locate the hole, but couldn't find it. Fortunately, because he didn't panic, he found a half-inch breathing-space between the river and the ice. He refilled his lungs, and finally found his escape hole.'

'Hair-raising, to say the least.' Dirk sounded genuinely impressed.

The miles clocked up on the jeep, and before too long Dirk said, 'Look over to the left—there are the Rockies, the best mountains in the whole world!'

Jane's eyes widened as she saw an endless stretch of grey rock appear on the horizon. 'They're magnificent. Quite awe-inspiring, and just like the spine of a sleeping prehistoric monster.'

'They've been around longer than those animals too,' Dirk remarked.

'They certainly look primeval. I can't wait to actually get to the National Park.' She knew she loved him when they were together like this.

'Then they'll look even more impressive, when you're right up close. They were formed by two great rock plates grinding up against one another—one here and the other on the base of the Pacific Ocean,' he told her.

At the toll-gate of the National Park, the keeper spotted Dirk's season ticket on his dashboard window, and waved them straight through.

Within a few hundred yards an intimidating rock face loomed by the edge of the road. Dirk

slowed the jeep, and as they rounded the bend
Jane saw a herd of mountain sheep surrounded
by a collection of tourists.

'This is where you meet your first mountain
creatures,' Dirk said. 'They're still wild, but the
sheep are canny enough to know they can get
an easy meal here.'

As soon as they had taken the bread from the
cooler in the back of the vehicle they were
surrounded by several older animals.

'They're almost tame,' Jane said in surprise,
as an older ram munched happily. Delicately
she stroked the top of his head. His thick curling
horns fascinated her.

The food was soon gone, and they they
watched the sure-footed creatures climb the
sheer face and mount the top of the rock. Some
loose stones became dislodged and splashed
into the tiny lake.

'How strange—the water's emerald-green.'
Jane looked puzzled. 'I thought the waters
would be blue to reflect the colour of the sky
today.'

'It's due to the minerals from the mountains,'
Dirk explained. 'They give the waters that deep
mysterious green, and this area is a frequent
haunt for the sheep—it's called a sheep lick.
The minerals are a necessary part of their diet.'

He leaned close. 'This is a tourist spot, and
far too crowded for us. I know a lake where it'll
be quite perfect for us to relax alone.'

They drove off the main road and took a wandering steep trail high into the mountains. They passed many beautiful lakes surrounded by pine cabins, but still Dirk drove on until the scenery became wilder.

'Here we are at last,' he grinned as he reversed the vehicle through a sandy trailway.

Jane jumped lightly down from the jeep, and the scene before her took her breath away. A short sandy beach led down to a glittering lake. Huge boulders flanked the shores on either side. To the left, the mountains rose proud and magnificent, and to the right tall lodgepole pine trees concealed the spot from the road.

'It's so peaceful and tranquil here.' She felt she should speak in a hushed voice. 'We could be the only people on the planet up here.' It was as if all her problems had vanished.

'Exactly.' Dirk caught her hand. 'The sheer grandeur of the place always makes me feel as if I have only a small part to play on earth. All the bustle of the hospital and the hassle of the city fade away here, and this is one place I feel I can really relax.'

They explored the shoreline, clambering over the great boulders, and all the while he held her hand fast.

Jane gazed down. 'The water's so pure and clear, you can look right down into the bottom—it's like looking through clear glass.'

'It's free of all pollution,' he explained.

Jane glanced up to the top of the towering mountains. 'Those wispy clouds look like curly locks of hair, they appear so fragile.'

'They're known as mares' tails, and they're made of ice crystals. Unfortunately. . .' he looked steadfastly into her eyes '. . .I have to be back in the city this evening, otherwise I'd show you how beautiful these clouds can be at sunset.'

It was as if he held her under a magical, sensual spell. All her misgivings and troubles vanished in his presence. Only the prospect of physical excitement now grew in her mind. Surely this was madness, but deep in her heart she wanted this man.

'Let's not waste this time,' said Dirk suddenly. 'Let's skinny-dip.'

'Swim in the nude?' Her voice rose slightly. She'd never done it before.

'Why not? You'll find it invigorating—I always do.' Without waiting for an answer he led her back to the jeep, opened the rear door and said, 'We can stow our clothes in here. That way, the sand won't get into them.'

Swiftly he sloughed off his cotton shirt. Then, without the slightest hesitancy, he unbuckled his jeans belt and slipped off his trousers and Y-fronts.

His magnificent body was tanned all over— he had obviously relaxed in this way many times before. As he threw his clothes haphaz-

ardly into the back of the jeep, he darted knowing glances at Jane, and the corner of his mouth
curved wickedly.

'I'll meet you in the water—don't be long.'

He strode off, completely at ease with his
nudity. And as she watched him wade powerfully into the shimmering depths of the lake
Jane couldn't deny that the sheer strength of his
body had a physical effect on her. His muscles
stood out in well-defined contours on his
shoulders, his belly and his thighs. He was a
man at one with the wilderness.

As he cut a fast crawl through the waters, his
potent power in action sent a ripple of excitement through her, and she discarded her
clothes quickly but neatly on top of the food
cooler.

Running full pelt into the lake, she dived in
headlong. The surge of the cold water chilled
her body. But within her core there burned the
desire for the man.

'It's brilliant!' she cried.

Dirk turned swiftly as her voice echoed
around the natural amphitheatre. Then he
began to swim, head down, purposefully
towards her. And suddenly he was gone, diving
deep beneath the surface.

She caught a glimpse of his submerged body
heading her way. His dark hair flowed out
behind him. Then he rose out of the water with

a great splash, and gripped her hard about her waist, pulling her on top of his body.

'Stay on top of me, and hold on fast around my neck,' he commanded. And in this position he ferried her to the shallows by some rocks. With an easy movement he set her on her feet, and she felt the waters swirling around the middle of her thighs.

'You're so beautiful, Jane,' he rasped. He held her tight against his body, and kissed her neck and her breasts.

The ecstasy of his caressing touch set her body on fire, and her hands trembled as she stroked the nape of his neck and his back. He was such a physically powerful man—she marvelled at the delicacy of his kisses, as his lips claimed her mouth. She felt the burn of desire course throught her whole body, as his kisses became deeper and his tongue probed and delighted her.

He was moulding her against the full length of his hard body. She felt as if she would melt against him. Then, reaching her fingers up into his damp thick hair, she was about to pull him even closer, when she felt something slide from her finger. Then she heard a splash.

A moan escaped her constricted throat. 'Oh, no. . .I think I've dropped my ring. Dirk, darling, stop a moment, please.'

She held his face in her hands, and gazed into his eyes.

'What's the matter, sweetheart?' His voice sounded choked through his ragged breathing.

'My grandmother's wedding-ring has slipped off my finger. It's at the bottom of the lake, just behind your left foot.'

He stared half comprehending, half dreamily at her. It was taking a little time for him to surface through his sensually induced drugged state.

'Your grandmother's ring?' He blinked forcibly. 'Where exactly did it drop?' He stepped back carefully enough, but disturbed the sandy bottom.

'Somewhere here. . .' Jane pointed with her big toe. And, peering, she gently began to feel for the ring with her foot.

'Keep your foot there on the spot,' he advised. 'I'll go under and see if I can find it. Rings are very important, and I wondered why you wore a wedding-band on your middle finger.'

He took several deep breaths and sank below. Jane had mixed feelings. Although it had felt so right, so wonderfully desirable to be in his arms, the loss of the ring would tinge this precious time with sadness.

Dirk remained submerged and sifted through the sand for what seemed like an eternity. As time ticked by, he exhaled gradually and bubbles of air broke on the surface, impeding her view.

He'll never find it, she thought desolately. I'm sure it's lost forever now.

But in the next instant he broke through the waters, the golden object held high above his head. 'Eureka!' he shouted.

'You're just fantastic.' She hugged him and wiped away the water from his drenched eyelashes. But when she tried to replace the ring her fingers were so cold that it was too big.

'Hmm. . .' Dirk looked serious. 'Where shall we put this for safe keeping? We haven't got a pocket between us.' He glanced down at his nudity, then his glance travelled slowly up hers.

She giggled.

'It'll be safe on my little finger. What do you say, Jane?'

'Yes, I like the idea.' She pushed it on to his left hand. 'There; it fits perfectly. And it's a good job you've got a lung capacity that's as large as Houdini's.'

'Not quite that excellent,' he smiled. 'But now that interruption is over let's carry on where we left off.'

Jane kissed him passionately; she was so thrilled with their time together. And soon she felt the rising heat of his potent manhood pressed firmly against her belly. Then she gasped as he nuzzled close to her neck and trailed his tongue down to her erect nipples.

She closed her eyes as the waves of sensuality engulfed her body and mind. Then as she slowly opened them again she saw an image over his right shoulder that made her freeze, and catch her breath.

The rear end of a black hairy hulk protruded from the jeep.

'It's a bear,' she whispered in high-pitched fear.

Sensing her sudden change, Dirk turned his head, then his whole body froze too. By this time the bear was growling in irritation.

'Whatever you do, stand perfectly still and don't move.' He turned silently in the water and put his body protectively between Jane and the wild creature.

She gulped and clung fiercely to Dirk. But she wanted to see what was happening, so she peeped round the side of his chest.

The bear's growls and snorts became louder. Jane couldn't think what he was doing in the back of the jeep—all the food was safely stowed away in the plastic cooler.

Then, to her horror, the creature bounded back and stood on its hind legs, surveying them directly. In his mouth was a frilly white garment.

I shall die of embarrassment before anything else, Jane thought. The creature eyed them for what seemed like an eternity, and she felt beads of sweat break out on her forehead.

Suddenly the bear shook its head, growled

angrily, and mercifully turned and romped off into the woods with the garment.

'Run with me—quick!' commanded Dirk, catching hold of her elbow and half dragging her through the water and up the beach. He wrenched open the front door of the jeep, and she jumped in. Slamming it behind her, he shouted, 'Lock it!'

He locked the back then raced round to his front door, and once safely inside they sat silent, wide-eyed and breathless.

'Thank God it was only a black bear,' gasped Dirk. 'They're relatively friendly, but like all wild creatures they're unpredictable.'

'The size of its claws were almost as big as my little fingers,' Jane gulped.

'That was a young one, only about five feet in height, and weighing about three hundred pounds. . . But what did it run off with that it was so excited about?'

'My frilly knickers'

To Jane's chagrin, Dirk leaned back and roared with laughter. 'Good God, that black bear was certainly living up to his nickname of the "playboy bear". And his mother should give him a severe spanking for that bad behaviour.'

'Spanking?' She looked amazed.

'Yes, mother bears do spank their cubs.'

'I'm still terrified,' she trembled. 'He might come back.'

Dirk put his arms around her wet body and

held her tight. 'Don't worry, sweetheart, we're perfectly safe in here. Put your clothes back on and we'll drive out of here.'

She leaned over the back of the seat and grabbed her remaining clothes. 'Damn him for running off with my knickers so publicly!'

Dirk tried unsuccessfully to hide a smile. 'If you're worried about wearing nothing under your jeans, I'll lend you my Y-fronts. But I don't think the cut is quite the same. . .hip-hugging or otherwise.'

'You still find it funny, but I'm frightened,' she threw back. 'The wilderness here in the mountains is as dangerous as any jungle!'

'You're safe with me,' he replied half teasingly, half reassuringly, 'And remember. . .me doctor, you Jane.'

She relaxed slightly, seeing the funny side. 'Well, I suppose I'm safe enough with a he-man who gives me bear-hugs.'

'Bear-hugs and the rest. We're going back to my log cabin now, where there won't be any animal interruptions.'

'Phew! This is some log cabin!' Jane exclaimed.

It was a huge L-shaped timber building, with two storeys and a veranda at the front. The roof was steeply sloping to allow the winter snow to slide off easily. A stone chimney was built on to the side, and the letter B was constructed in reddish stones amid lighter beige ones, stamping the Blackwell name on to the building. It was a bold, extravagant brand, like Dirk himself.

Jane was dressed only in her jeans and T-shirt—she hadn't had the time to put on her shoes. And Dirk had only bothered to slip on his jeans. This building is just as impressive as he is, she thought. It blended perfectly with its surroundings. Behind it loomed the mountains, sheer, wild and immovable.

Dirk unlocked and opened the front door, allowing her to pass through first. 'I promised you tea in the mountains, and that's exactly what you will have,' he told her.

He led her through to the kitchen. Although spacious and full of every modern gadget, it was gorgeously panelled with natural woods.

Opening a high cupboard, he scanned its contents. 'Now, would you like tea, or coffee, or iced lemonade or——?'

The excitement of their time at the lake still ebbed through Jane's body, but the fear had completely gone. Feeling safe and secure in the Blackwell cabin, she slid her arms round his waist and said, 'I'd love the "or".'

He turned quickly and bright lights in his eyes glinted. 'Ah, that's what I so like about you, Jane. You're a woman who knows exactly what you want.'

He stroked the soft hair off her forehead. His kisses were light and gently. The old desire flamed within her again, as he pushed her hair aside and stroked the nape of her neck. Shudders of delicious sensation brought her body acutely alive.

'Your hair is still damp, sweetheart,' he murmured close to her ear. 'Let's take a shower and get to know each other even better.'

'Yes. . .let's. . .' she answered dreamily.

She hardly noticed the sumptuous bathroom fittings; she had eyes only for Dirk. But as she neared the bath she stopped dead in her tracks.

'There's a spider, and it's as big as a saucer,' she croaked as her stomach churned at the sight.

'Not another critter threatening to ruin our love life!' Dirk ground out. 'I'll soon sort this one out.'

She caught his arm before he could do anything. 'Don't kill it—I couldn't bear it if you squashed it. Even if it is such a horrible-looking creature, it's got feelings.'

'All right—don't panic.' He reached for a glass that was sitting on a shelf above a handbasin. Jane's stomach churned as he carefully placed the glass over the creature.

'I can't help it,' she said in a choked voice. 'But spiders are so weird, with their eyes on stalks.'

'I'll soon get it out of the cabin. There's a piece of flexible cardboard in this cupboard; I'll just slide it underneath and then I can put the spider out of the window.'

She watched from a safe distance as Dirk gently manipulated the cardboard and transported the creature to the window. A shiver ran down her spine, as she saw it fall on to the veranda below, then scuttle away.

'Even though I don't like them, I'm glad you didn't hurt it,' she said. 'And then you never know—it might be a reincarnation.'

'Reincarnation?' He raised one black eyebrow sceptically. 'What do you think it's reincarnated from? An octopus from the sea-bed, or a clumsy circus juggler?'

The adrenalin was still pumping throughout Jane's body. 'Huh! I suppose you don't believe in reincarnation because it hasn't been proved by your precious scientific principles?'

He surveyed her darkly, but it was only for an instant. 'I have no intention of belittling other people's beliefs,' he assured her.

'It would surprise me if you did believe in it!' she shot back. Quarrels with his father flashed into her mind. She tried to quell them, but it was no good. Sometimes the past got the better of her. 'I suppose you might like the idea because you think you could come back to earth as a soaring eagle?'

He considered her for a moment, looking down at her from his lofty height. 'Nothing so superior. If I had the choice, I'd come back as a bed-bug.'

She stared at him wide-eyed. 'Why?' There was something about his look that made her wary.

'I'm basing my judgement on our track record of trying to make love. It seems that I end up as a frantic romantic every time, but the animals have the upper hand. Now, if I were a bed-bug, I could easily snuggle up to you, and in the most intimate places.'

'Facetious bastard!' she shot back. She hated him for amusingly scoring off her. 'I'll make sure I sleep with a can of pest repellent on my bedside table from now on.' She was at flash-point now, and the past got the better of her once again. 'And I'd like my ring back, please. It belonged to my father's mother.'

The ring was stuck firmly and as Dirk twisted and turned it for what seemed like an eternity Jane's temper rose even higher. 'Give it to me now.' She felt exasperated.

He glared at her through narrow, glittering eyes. 'With pleasure, madam.'

He continued to struggle with it, only to annoy Jane to bursting-point.

'I don't know why I let you wear it in the first place,' she sounded off recklessly. 'Especially after your father's——'

'My father's what?' he demanded.

'I should have sued him, started proceedings

long ago——' Jane was blinded by pain and rage now.

With a mighty wrench Dirk tore the ring free and thrust it towards her. 'Here it is, for God's sake, you stupid, revengeful girl. I'd like you to know that *my* father has just had to take early retirement because of high blood-pressure. And that was because he overworked, and no doubt pestering from the likes of you didn't help!'

'But you still have your father——'

'Stop this at once!' Dirk ground out. 'Seeing you in this light has opened my eyes, Jane. If I had any feelings for you at all, they've vanished now. Your need for this ridiculous revenge has quashed everything. We're going back to the city immediately, and our relationship from now on will be purely professional!'

CHAPTER SEVEN

THE drive back to the city had been a sullen and silent affair for both Jane and Dirk. And as soon as she left him the full error of her foolish words hit her forcefully.

She had cried and cried into her pillow on succeeding nights, bitterly regretting what she had said in temper.

The time in the mountains at the lake had been a heady, electrifying sensual experience, more thrilling than any other time she had spent with a man. And Dirk had defended her, put his body between herself and the black bear. What more could she want from any man?

Ah, and how had she repaid him? She'd thrown up the old conflict of her father's death and hit him where it hurt. In the light of time elapsed and rational thinking, she was ashamed.

The knowledge that Dirk's father was in poor health, and the obvious worry it caused, made her feel dreadful. She wanted to offer Dirk comfort at this worrying time. Her father's words that any revenge would only hurt *her* rang clearly in her head. He had been so right.

Unfortunately she hardly saw Dirk, except

when they had to discuss patients, and at these times he was always cool and remote. This deepened her heartache, and made her feel that all was lost. There was only work.

Graham Walker had just started a three-week vacation in Europe, so his list had been divided among the physios of the outpatient team.

Jane had inherited a twenty-nine-year-old labourer called Jake Malpass. He was one of Dirk's patients and had been diagnosed as mechanical low back pain.

This morning Jane would have to go through a detailed back assessment before treating him. He had been unable to attend for his initial appointment with Graham, but had rung to explain that he had a previous appointment with the workers' compensation board.

At five to eleven Jane was sitting in the outpatients' office filling in the attendance register, when she heard a message over the intercom. Her new patient had arrived.

She was surprised to watch the man walk briskly into the waiting area, sit down easily, and lean forward to read a newspaper.

Curious, she thought. He doesn't look as though he has any back problems at the moment. But perhaps he had just suffered a muscle strain, and now the effects had eased.

Dirk's diagnosis was obviously right. Jake was sitting and leaning even further forward now. And in this position there was the greatest pressure on the intervertebral discs.

From the rolled-up sleeve of his T-shirt, Jake withdrew a packet of cigarettes. Having lit one, he took a satisfying drag, then turned easily to dispose of the smoking match in the sandy substance of a large free-standing ashtray.

Hmm, nothing much wrong with his muscles or his movements, Jane mused. From the looks of things this might prove to be an easy treatment.

After she had introduced herself she escorted Jake to one of the cubicles with a hydraulic plinth. But as soon as Jake met her he began to hold his back very stiffly, as if guarding it. And he walked with a pronounced limp.

'It's the pain down the back of my left leg,' he explained as he sat down awkwardly on a chair. 'It's giving me real gyp.'

Jane resisted the idea to write him down as a malingerer from the start—after all, she hadn't gone through her thorough examination.

As she took the past history she came to some pertinent questions. 'How exactly did you injure your back?' she asked him.

'Oh, I remember all right. It came on suddenly when I was lifting boxes in a small awkward space. I had to lift and twist and turn—I told the company it was bad for backs. But of course they wouldn't do anything about it. And

I just had to get on with the job to earn an honest dollar.'

Jane asked many more questions and jotted down her findings. Jake was very forthcoming with his answers; some of them, especially relating to the type of duration of pain, he recited off parrot-fashion.

When all the exhaustive history had been taken, she said, 'I'll need to do a physical examination now. So slip off all your clothes except your underpants, then lie on the plinth.'

He stood up stiffly and took his weight on his right leg while flexing his left one up and down. 'It catches me out when I've been sitting a while,' he said.

Jane wanted to watch his movements while he undressed, but unfortunately she was called to the telephone in the office. And when she returned to Jake she entered the cubicle to find a shocking surprise. Jake was lying on the plinth stark naked.

Keeping her eyes riveted on his face, she said calmly, 'Put your underpants back on—complete nudity won't be necessary for this examination. I'll be back in a few minutes.'

As she made a hasty exit and walked back to the office, she raised her eyes to heaven. What a pity Graham was on holiday. And he was the only male physio in the department!

Fortunately eleven o'clock was a very busy

time, so she doubted that Jake would have any opportunity to make any sort of pass.

It was most unusual for any male patients to take any sort of sexual advantage. But somehow Jane had a very cautious feeling about this patient.

In the office she related the incident to some of the other physios, and they decided to give her some moral back-up by constantly coming in and out of Jake's treatment cubicle on the pretext that they were looking for some machine or piece of equipment.

Jake tried not to look peeved when Jane re-entered the cubicle, and she put on her most cool professional face, as if nothing untoward had happened.

Going through the whole examination proved a difficult task.

'I can't do that movement—everything's painful,' Jake continually complained.

It became plainer and plainer to Jane that no consistent pattern of underlying pathology was present.

'Can you bend your hip and your knee up towards your tummy while I give a little resistance?' she asked him.

'It's hard to even bend the knee. . .no, no, I can't do anything even when you push slightly.'

Jane guided his leg and laid it carefully back on the plinth. A few minutes ago he had been able to lift his knee up and down while standing, and then the movement had been against gravity, which was much more difficult than in the lying position. Here gravity was counterbalanced and therefore the movement should have been easier.

Just then Helen Davis, one of the younger physios, popped her head through the cubicle curtains. 'Have you got the ultrasound machine in here?' she queried.

'No—sorry.' Jane turned and tried to hide a smile. She knew her friend was keeping an eye on her.

Next Jane put her one hand beneath the heel of Jake's painful leg and her other one beneath his thigh. 'Let me lift your leg up,' she said.

She had hardly lifted the foot eight inches off the plinth when he cried out and made a great show of grabbing the back of his leg.

'Can't do that, girl. It's my sciatica, you know—my sciatic nerve's being made worse by the slipped disc.'

He seemed to have this diagnosis firmly lodged in his mind. And he was correct in saying this, because the problem was related to this test.

'Sorry, I'll lower your leg a little.' Using her words as a distraction, Jane hardly moved the leg, but pushed Jake's foot upwards.

If he had really been suffering from pressure on part of the sciatic nerve then this would have stretched the nerve even more, and caused greater pain. However, he showed no sign.

It was as if he had found out something about the pathology of the back, and was now playing it to great effect. Very few patients did this. But some were canny enough to know that the back was such a complicated mechanism, and they might get away with it. And for such disability remuneration from the compensation board was pretty high.

She next went on to another manoeuvre to test for a malingerer. This was the Hoover test. Standing at the base of the plinth, she cupped her hands beneath his heels.

'Try and lift your left leg now,' she told him.

Jake puffed out his cheeks as if making a great effort. 'Can't do it, girl. Can't do it.'

But Jane knew he wasn't making any real effort, because there was no downward pressure from his right heel on to her hand.

When she had finished her examination, she said, 'I'll need to give you some deep heat with the short-wave diathermy machine—this will bring more blood to the part and help it to heal.'

He sniffed a bit, and looked sceptical.

'But you'll have to move into the next cubicle where the plinth is lower,' she added.

'Haven't you been pushing that pedal and raising me up and down on this table for the last half-hour?' he threw back caustically.

'Yes, but the short wave is a deep-heat

machine that throws out a certain amount of radiation, and because the plinth is made of metal parts it might get hot and give you a burn.' She hoped she'd blind him with science.

'Oh, all right. . .' Grumpily he hobbled through into the next cubicle.

Jane was certain he was malingering to some extent so that he could increase his compensation claim; however, he might have a slight lesion somewhere, so she decided not to give the deepest short wave because if this heated a protruding intervertebral disc this selective heating might cause expansion of the soft tissues and could cause more pressure on the nerve and therefore more pain.

So she opted for the drum. This was an applicator in three hinged parts that contained a cable in a plastic case, which could be moulded to the shape of the patient.

She was careful to put a thick terry towel between Jake's back and the drum, and several felt spacers with holes between the cables and the side of the plinth.

'When the machine is switched on, it will feel like a comfortable warmth,' she explained. 'Whatever you do, don't move and touch the machine, because you might get a burn.'

'How can I turn and touch it?' he said. 'You've put it miles away.' He reached out his arm awkwardly and flicked one of the cables.

'Now that's exactly what you don't do,' she

cautioned. Above all things, she didn't want
him to get a burn. He was just the sort to sue!
'Even these cables give out radiation. I'll prove
it to you.'

She left the cubicle and came back with an
ordinary household light in the shape of a
fluorescent tube.

'Now you've seen plenty of these lights
before, haven't you?'

Jake nodded.

'Well, I'll make it light up without plugging it
in just by putting it near the cable.'

'I'll believe it when I see it,' he shrugged.

'Wait until I switch on the machine.' She
turned all the dials to zero, as was standard
practice, then switched on the machine and
turned up the intensity until Jake said he felt a
comfortable heat.

From the corner of his eye he could see her
place the fluorescent tube near the cable. Suddenly it lit up and glowed brightly.

'That's a wonder!' he gasped.

'Yes, it's just like magic,' Jane laughed.

She left him with the instruction to ring a
nearby bell if the heat should feel too hot. Then
she went to another patient.

After his heat treatment, Jake seemed a little
more docile, and Jane taught him some gentle
exercises. Then they agreed on the time of the
next treatment on the following day.

But Jake didn't turn up for his appointment

the next day, nor did he ring to give an explanation. Jane tried to contact him on several occasions as time passed, but without success.

It was Sunday afternoon, and the air in Jane's little apartment was oppressively hot. Even though every window was opened to its fullest extent, still the heat beat up from the outside car park in great shimmering waves.

She longed to be free from the city. If only she could be back in the mountains with Dirk. Then she would re-enact those scenes, and she would never quarrel with him.

Now she felt that he was irretrievably lost to her, and this left an almost unbearable emptiness.

Fairlock Park was a twenty-minute walk away, so she set off briskly. By the time she reached the park she felt thirsty, so she tagged on to the end of a queue at one of the concessions stands. When her turn came she asked for a lemonade.

'Make that two, please.' Dirk's deep voice came from nowhere.

Turning quickly, Jane looked up into that handsome face that caused her so much heartache. 'I'm only ordering lemonade.' She felt confused. 'And it's usually half filled with slushy ice.'

'Then that's perfect for a hot afternoon in the

sun.' He paid for the drinks and led the way to a nearby picnic table.

They sat side by side in the shade of a Douglas fir. Jane sipped her lemonade tentatively. Really she wanted to make the peace.

She began falteringly, staring down at her drink. 'I. . . I'm so sorry about the way I behaved to you in the mountains. I would never have sued your father. . .' Great tears began to roll down her cheeks.

She felt the unbearable silence between them like a chasm, then his large, warm hand closed over hers.

'You spoke in anger, and because you're still deeply hurt, Jane.' She heard his sigh. 'My mother died years ago, and I still haven't got over it fully. But then my father and I spent a lot of time talking it out. That's what helps—it does ease the pain.'

His arm slid about her shoulder, and she leaned gratefully into him.

'You're right,' she agreed between sobs. 'It's just that it seems such an enormous obstacle.'

'Then we'll take it stage by stage. Perhaps right now we should just enjoy the park and the sunshine together. I know I remind you of my father, but if our relationship is to grow I feel we must start confronting the problem.'

He tipped her face up so that he was looking directly into her eyes. 'I don't want to lose you, Jane. We have something special deep down, and if we can overcome this we'll be even stronger together.'

Dirk was such a lovely man, she couldn't bear to lose him. 'Yes, I'll try anything,' she agreed, snuggling closer, and then as his strong arms enfolded her and she felt his deep, steady breathing she began to relax.

When he was aware that her emotions had subsided, he took her hand between both of his and said, 'Let's walk by the river. The sound of the water is always soothing.'

He led the way, still holding her close with his arm around her waist. Gradually Jane relaxed further, then she became aware of the people. One man in particular caught her eye.

He was a man in his thirties, dressed in a skimpy pair of shorts that appeared to be the sole support of his beer belly. He reminded her of Jake Malpass. Because she had the distinct feeling that her patient would pose a problem she brought up the subject.

'Graham is on holiday, so I've inherited one of his patients,' she began. 'I think he's a——'

She would have said the word 'phoney', but suddenly a feeling of intense panic gripped her mind. Before her father had died, these feelings had invaded her mind in the same way. Now she stood still, and half covered her face with her free hand.

Instantly Dirk tightened his grip. 'What's the

matter? Has the sun got to you? Do you feel faint?'

'No. . .no. . . It's not me.' She shook her head. 'But someone is in trouble. I can feel it. . . It's as if water is rushing all about them.' She lifted her head to look over the little hill between the park and the river. 'Yes, someone's in the water and they're in trouble!'

The feeling was so overwhelmingly real that she ran straight up the hill, and from the advantage of its summit quickly scanned the shore and the waterline below.

'There's a girl in the shallows! She's fallen,' she cried.

Dirk had kept abreast of Jane as she ran. He raced ahead down the sandy eroded embankment, and out to the girl.

Jane felt the loose sand giving way under her feet as she followed. She was half afraid, half elated. Her premonition of danger had been correct, but fortunately it hadn't been related to drowning.

'I'm a doctor,' said Dirk briskly as he helped the girl on to dry land, 'and Jane here is one of my physios. Tell me your name, and exactly what happened.'

The girl was pretty and about sixteen, with well made-up eyes. But her make-up had become smudged by her tears. 'My name is Jill, and I caught my foot between some of the larger stones and fell awkwardly. Now the outside of my ankle really hurts and it's beginning to swell.'

Dirk squatted down by his patient and gently palpated the outside of her ankle. 'Yes, you've certainly done some damage there, young lady. It already feels hot. Have you tried to stand on it?'

'Yes, but I couldn't take the weight through it.'

He lifted her on to the bank and explained, 'Spraining the ankle is a very common injury. Let me take a closer look now.'

Gently he went through five passive movements at the ankle joint, two passive movements at the talo-calcaneal joint, six passive movements at the mid-tarsal joint, then he completed four resisted foot movements.

After some final palpation which made Jill wince slightly, he said, 'I think you've torn a few fibres of the ligament on the outside of your ankle. But until we've had an X-ray to check you out we'll treat your foot as if one of the bones is actually broken. It's just a precaution, but sometimes a part of the fibula, the lateral malleolus, can have become avulsed or broken away when the ligament was stressed.'

Jill looked reassured by his explanation, then Dirk carried her to one of the nearby picnic tables and set her on the bench with her leg in elevation to prevent further swelling.

'It's important to keep the foot up,' he

explained, 'otherwise you'll get more swelling in your tissues, and that could lead to further problems later on.'

Turning to Jane, he said, 'I'll go and get the jeep and some of my first-aid equipment. I've got a chemical cold pack, but I'd rather use ice if I could get it.'

'Try the little shop where we bought the lemonade,' Jane suggested. 'They're bound to have loads there.'

'Good thinking; I'll be back as soon as I can.'

Jane turned her attention back to her patient. 'Are your friends somewhere here in the park, Jill?' she asked.

The girl began to cry and rub her eyes. 'No. . . I came with my boyfriend, but we had a row, and he told me I could walk home. I wish I hadn't rowed with him, even if I've always thought that making up afterwards was worth it.'

'Someone at the hospital will give him a ring, if you like,' Jane ventured.

Some minutes later Dirk drove up, jumped out, opened the back door and hurried over with his emergency equipment.

'You're in luck, Jill. I've got plenty of flaked ice to prevent further swelling, and the ladies in the shop very kindly soaked this elastic bandage in cold water too.'

As he applied the pressure bandage around the perimeter of the ankle, he went on to explain, 'This will decrease any internal bleeding.'

Meanwhile Jane folded the flaked ice inside a couple of tea-towels that the shop had also supplied. And when Jill was safely installed in the back of the jeep, with her leg still in elevation, Jane encased her foot in the ice.

Jill looked down at her foot. 'It looks the queerest thing, all bandaged in tea-towels. But it does take some of the pain away.' She laughed. 'When I'm at the hospital, will I get the ultrasound the professional footballers are always having?'

Dirk drove smoothly out of the park. 'We'll have to see what your X-ray plates look like first. If the ligament is only slightly torn then you'll have ultrasound. But not for the first forty-eight hours, because the high-frequency sound waves would only vibrate the soft tissues, and that could cause more bleeding.'

At the emergency department of the general hospital Dirk organised Jill's X-rays immediately, while Jane took the patient's provincial health care card, and gave the numbers to the clerk. She also phoned the boyfriend.

Fortunately Dirk's diagnosis proved to be correct and Jill had no bone injury. So he strapped her ankle with athletic tape, and Jane taught her how to use a pair of crutches without putting her foot to the ground.

Dirk then wrote out a prescription for physio.

Jill opted to attend the university hospital because it was nearer to her home.

When Dirk had finished writing up Jill's notes at a desk in Emergency, he sighed and looked at Jane. 'They say a doctor's never off duty, and it was a piece of luck that you heard Jill's cries for help when you did.'

'I didn't hear her cry out. I just had a strange feeling. Just an overpowering sensation that someone was in danger. . .like a premonition,' she told him.

He raised one black eyebrow sceptically, and she knew that he was about to argue on his old scientific principles. So much for their agreement to talk out their problems rationally.

Suddenly a charge nurse called out, 'Dr Blackwell! Your father's on the phone. He wants to know if you've forgotten to pick him up at the international airport.'

'Damn it, so I did! Excuse me a moment, Jane.'

Dirk walked over to the extension and she heard him talking and laughing with his father. And when he returned he asked gently, 'Would you like to meet my father, Jane? As the opportunity has arisen I think it might be a good idea!'

But, even after all their rational talk, Jane's throat became dry and she stammered, 'No. . . no, it's too early. . . I can't. . .you're asking too much.'

Dirk's face became strained and his voice low. 'You must confront this, sweetheart. The problem won't just go away.'

She shook her head. 'Not now. . .give me time?'

He caught her hands and imprisoned them firmly. 'Yes, now, Jane. The sooner you do this, the sooner the problem will go away.'

She fought to extricate herself from his hold, but he held her tighter. 'Trust me, Jane—trust me. The path to resolution is yours alone.'

'No. . .not now.' The emotions were winning again, and she hardly knew what she was saying.

She caught a tremor in his voice. 'All right, it's too soon, but you must agree to a meeting some time, because we can't go on unless this is resolved.'

Now all she wanted to do was run away. 'Yes, yes, another time, I promise.'

When she was alone her emotions subsided. When it had come to the crunch, her nerve had failed. But another time she would have to be prepared. If she wasn't she risked losing Dirk, and she didn't know if she could bear that.

CHAPTER EIGHT

FOR the rest of the weekend Jane's mind was in a turmoil concerning Dirk. But she had to put all this on hold when she was treating patients.

When Harry Adamski walked into the wax treatment area on Monday morning he was carrying a large black suitcase. And Jane could have sworn that he gave Sister Veronica a very special smile.

'Hi, everyone.' He bent to stow the case under the table. 'I'm a happy man today, because starting next month I'll be working again.'

Jane was busily tying the tapes of a blanket mitt around Sister Veronica's wrist. 'That's brilliant,' she said.

'I'm so very pleased for you, Harry.' Sister Veronica added, 'What sort of job is it?'

He stepped up to the wax bath and dipped his hand in. 'I'm going to be a crane operator.'

'That's great,' enthused Jane. 'You won't have to do the heavy lifting—the machine will do all the work.'

Harry continued, 'It's a fantastic feeling. I'll be high up in the sky, manipulating really complex sets of levers. It means being as deft and precise as I am when I'm conjuring.'

While Jane put a plastic wrapping around Harry's hand, Sister Veronica sat down at the table and Jane noticed that when she looked at Harry her face was quite radiant.

Jane's curiosity was aroused, but she had to leave her two patients for their twenty-minute heat treatment, because she had to work on somebody else. And as she left the area she saw that their heads were locked together in some sort of animated conference.

They're plotting something, for sure, she thought. Now, I wonder what that black suitcase has got to do with it?

Her individual patient took longer to treat than she had anticipated. So by the time she got back to Harry and Sister Veronica she was pleased to see that they had peeled off the wax themselves and gone through their exercises.

'Well done, you two. You don't appear to have missed me at all today,' she laughed.

'We guessed you were busy,' grinned the nun. 'And we've been here so many weeks now, we could almost do these exercises in our sleep.'

The trio then made their way to the gym for the advanced part of their treatment. While Jane set Sister Veronica up on spring resistance, Harry started work on the Westminster pulley system. Jane checked her two model patients as they worked away with gusto.

'Slow down a bit, Harry,' she advised. 'You're

clattering those weights about too quickly. It'll take more muscle work if you let them down slowly.'

'Sorry, Jane. But I feel so good doing the work now. There's no pain at all, not even the slightest jarring.'

He completed another set, then looked at his watch and asked rather shyly, 'Do you think Sister Veronica and I could leave a bit early today, please?'

Ah, now it's coming, thought Jane. 'What's all the hurry about?' She tried to keep the teasing tone out of her voice.

'I've agreed to do a lunchtime magic session for some of the younger children at Sister's school. I've brought all my formal wear in a suitcase—you know, white tie and tails. But it takes a bit of time to get all togged up in them . . .could I use a cubicle to change now?'

Jane was nonplussed for a moment. It had been firmly lodged in her mind that they were about to elope or something.

'Yes, please let us go early,' intervened the nun. 'The children are so looking forward to seeing Harry—they've heard so much about him.'

'All right,' laughed Jane. 'I don't see how I can refuse. Anyway, you'll be continuing with your exercises when you perform, Harry.'

She tidied away the weights and the spring resistance equipment, then walked back

towards the wax area. She had a sneaking desire
to see Harry all dressed up to perform. But as
she was passing through the main cubicle section she bumped into Dirk.

'Ah, Jane. . .you're the very person I was
looking for.'

Her heart lurched as he led her to a quiet
area.

'How are you feeling today?' he asked. 'You
were a bit worked up when we parted.'

'I'm fine now—it was just the surprise element. How is your father?'

She saw that her question pleased him. 'I'm
glad to see you're able to think of him too. It
shows me you're forgiving.'

In time, Jane thought, and swallowed hard.
She still didn't know how she'd react to the
actual meeting.

Dirk continued, 'My father looks well, but he
needs taking out of himself. Time hangs too
heavily on him without his work. But he's
looking forward to visiting his brother in BC.
They'll go fishing in the mountains——'

He stopped in mid-sentence, and looked up
in astonishment as Sister Veronica and Harry
walked by. They had obviously shared some
joke together, because they were chuckling.
And they had eyes for no one else.

Dirk's riveted gaze followed the pair as they
walked towards the exit. 'Those two certainly
make a stunning couple,' he remarked. 'The

nun is strikingly beautiful even in her habit. But who's that young man dressed to impress any débutante at a coming-out ball? I feel a bit disorientated. . .it is the middle of the day, isn't it?'

'That's your patient, Harry Adamski,' grinned Jane.

'Mother Superior! And heavens above!' Dirk bent closer to her ear and lowered his voice seductively. 'Now what sort of treatment in the physio department has changed our Harry so drastically? And made a depressed young man strut his stuff like that!' He lifted his left hand and started to enumerate on his fingers. 'Was it the swishing whirlpool treatment? Or the soothing wax that makes your hands feel so smooth? Pumping iron in the gym? Or. . .' He looked directly at Jane and with the most serious expression. 'Or nun of the above?'

Jane nearly collapsed in giggles. She knew Dirk was trying to lighten her mood. 'I think there's been some celestial intervention,' she told him.

'Exactly. . .' Dirk shrugged his shoulders. 'Final rehabilitation comes in many forms.'

'Actually, Harry's on his way to give a performance of magic for the children at Sister Veronica's school,' she explained.

'Abracadabra and all that, eh? Hmm. . .' He looked at her steadily, mischief glinting in his eyes. 'How would you like supper with me tomorrow evening? And I promise some after-dinner entertainment.'

'What ideas have you got up your sleeve?' she queried.

'Nothing as professional as our Harry. But it will be mysterious and surprising.'

'In that case I'd love to come. What time?'

'I'll pick you up around seven-thirty. Oh, and don't wear anything too formal.'

Their banter had put Jane off her guard. Suddenly she felt nervous and gulped, 'Will I be meeting your father?'

'No. This interlude will be just for the two of us.'

Ten minutes before Jake Malpass's appointment time Jane was half hoping that he wouldn't show up. She knew there would be a confrontation about his missed treatments. She still hadn't been able to reach him on the telephone, and according to the regulations she should really write him a letter advising him that his treatments would be terminated if he did not make contact.

His appointment time came and went. So Jane pulled out a sheet of hospital headed notepaper and began to write. This proved to have an undesirable effect, because she glanced up and saw Jake walk into the waiting area. Raising her eyebrows, she pushed the piece of paper away and walked out of her office.

'Hello, Jake. You've missed a few appointments here. What was the problem?'

'The damned treatment! That was the problem,' he snapped.

Jane felt her heart sinking.

He continued, 'It was all that pulling about—it just made me worse, girl. And as for those exercises. . .I couldn't do any. I've been laid up in bed for days.'

'I tried to ring you at home, and contact you.' Jane spoke as evenly as she could.

Glibly he replied, 'The phone is downstairs—I couldn't make it all that way.'

She sighed inwardly. 'Well, let's take a look at you now you're here, Jake, and see how we can alter your treatment.'

'Something's got to alter,' he grumbled on. 'I can't stand this pain for much longer. I can't sleep.'

It was true that the tissues under his eyes were black and puffy. But Jane really wondered if that might be the result of successive nights on the town. His breath smelt of strong peppermint. Was that to disguise the smell of alcohol?

She went through a simple examination in the cubicle, but was constantly interrupted by mumblings and grumblings.

'I think I'll try you on a moist hot pack today,' she decided. 'Some patients don't react well to the short wave, so we'll try this alternative.'

As she prepared the pack on the work bench

by the hydrocalator, she mentally reviewed her patient. She had been very careful about choosing the type of short wave that she had given him on his first treatment. But perhaps even that was too deep. The hot pack would be soothing, and couldn't possibly do him any harm because the heating effect was more superficial.

Jane needn't have worried about the effects of the moist heat, because when she entered the cubicle to check Jake five minutes after she had set him on the hot pack she found him snoring.

But when the full heat treatment was up he was fully awake and back to his old moaning. He coughed as he laboriously rolled over on to his back for the simple exercises.

'Coughing's dreadful,' he complained. 'It brings on that sharp pain down my leg.'

'I think we'll leave the exercises for today,' Jane decided. 'That way we'll see if the hot pack has any good and lasting effect. Would this time tomorrow be all right for your next appointment?'

'I should think so. Yes, I'll be here. I do want to get better, you know.'

She rather doubted this as they said goodbye. Then she left the cubicle and returned to the office.

Helen Davis, one of the younger physios, spoke up. 'I thought you'd discharged Jake

Malpass because he hadn't bothered to show up for so many treatments?'

'Nearly,' replied Jane. 'But he turned up today, so I haven't got that excuse. I think he's only coming so that he can tell Dr Blackwell it's quite useless.'

'Huh!' Helen looked disapproving. 'I should have told you earlier, but it quite slipped my mind.' She lowered her voice as they watched Jake hobble out of the department. 'I'm sure I saw him last Saturday night. It was very late when my boyfriend and I were coming out of a club downtown. I could only see by the street-lights, but I was almost certain that he was your patient. And he was crouching down changing the tyre on his car quite easily.'

'That doesn't surprise me.' Jane shook her head. 'But you say you couldn't be absolutely sure?'

'Sorry—it was nearly one in the morning. But if I were putting on a bet I'd put down quite a bit of money.'

Jane had felt intrigued by the evening Dirk had promised. Now she was feeling relaxed and mellow as she munched her after-dinner mint and sipped the last of her black coffee in his apartment.

'Let's relax on the chesterfield. It's more comfortable there.' He took her hand gently and led her across the room.

Her body sank into the soft leather uphol-
stery. Drawing her close, he kissed her, and the
delicacy of his touch made her glow inside. He
kissed her eyes reverently.

'Ah, Jane,' he sighed. 'I've been longing to be
close to you like this for what seems like a
millennium. Your pupils are wonderfully large
and dilated now, and I know there's no trickery
behind your responses.'

'Trickery?' She looked at him curiously.

'In the Middle Ages some unscrupulous
women used to impregnate their eyes with
belladonna. The drug dilates the pupils artificially, and this has always been a turn-on for
men.'

She stroked his dark eyebrows with her fingertips. His eyes were deeply dilated too. And
now he reminded her of the first time they had
met at the Old-Timers' Cabin. She could feel the
tension in his muscles, and she knew he was
holding his excitement in check.

'So this is your idea of after-dinner entertainment, Dr Blackwell. . .' She spoke softly but
mock-teasingly.

Dirk chuckled deep in his throat. 'I've been
polishing my skills for this performance for a
long time.'

She could see him trying not to smile, as he
pulled a small white card from his left breast
pocket.

'Three very special words are written here on

this card. I wonder if you can unravel the mystery, Jane?'

She took the card and studied it. 'Is it a foreign language?' she queried.

'No, a universal one.'

She looked at the letters, again trying to fathom the sense of it: *ECN A MOR*

'I give up,' she laughed.

'Never give up on this,' he said seriously. 'I want you to study the words while I go away and prepare for the rest of the evening.'

She opened her eyes wide. What had he been planning in his deep, devious mind?

'Now promise you'll be good, and wait for me here. I might take a few minutes before I come back.'

'You're full of intrigue!' she smiled.

'Promise?'

'Yes, I promise. And I'll study your strange little card.'

It was hard for Jane to sit and wait. Really, she longed to follow Dirk. But he had obviously prepared for tonight, and taken a great deal of trouble.

When he returned he made what could only be called an entrance.

'That's not fair!' she cried. 'You distinctly told me to wear something informal—that's why I'm wearing this short silk dress. And you. . .you're so formal, you could be about to attend a first night at the opera.'

He looked more devastatingly handsome than ever before. He was wearing a black evening suit, with satin-faced lapels, and his white bow-tie was knotted neatly at his throat. And to crown the effect he wore a black top hat.

'Sit back and relax. I may only deceive you with magic tonight, but my real aim right here and now is to amaze and entertain you.'

'Ah, now I understand,' smiled Jane. 'You're all dressed up Harry Adamski style.'

'Just like the great magicians,' he continued, taking off his top hat and making a deep bow. 'I'm going to baffle and enthrall you.'

From behind a Japanese screen in the room he withdrew a stand and a small high table. After placing his top hat on the table, he turned back to Jane.

'Have you fathomed out the riddle of the three magic words?' he asked.

She looked down at the card. 'I'm afraid they're a mystery to me.'

'By the end of the evening all will be revealed, and I hope you'll understand.' He took the card and placed it on top of the stand.

By now she was really curious, and she was sure his patter was full of riddles.

'All good conjurors can work with cards,' he began. 'And close-up magic is definitely on the agenda for us tonight. But there are too many cards in a standard pack, so I'll just choose a few.'

He held his right arm straight out to the side, and pulled his cuff up. 'As you can see, there's nothing up my sleeve.'

He turned his hand in the air, and from nowhere produced a joker.

'Where did that come from?' Jane genuinely sounded amazed.

'It was magicked out of the air, of course.' He used a mysterious voice that made her laugh. 'But tonight the entertainment will have a serious value. So I'll throw the joker into my top hat.' He discarded it deftly.

Turning his hand again, he said, 'Now, what have we here?'

'The Queen of Hearts,' she replied.

'Yes, every man should have a lady in his life, and in his heart.' He discarded this card too.

But however hard Jane peered at his hands she could have sworn there was nothing concealed there.

Dirk produced a third card. 'And here's the King of Hearts. But he wants to be with the Queen, so we'll put them together.'

'I bet you've got an ace up your sleeve too,' she laughed.

'How did you know that?' And from out of nowhere came the Ace of Hearts. 'When entertaining a young lady, it's essential for a man to have a red ace about his body.' He looked very knowing as he held this card.

And she knew he meant it to have some

sensual significance. By now, she was totally fascinated and spellbound, as Dirk produced fans of cards from nowhere and dropped them into the top hat.

'Brilliant!' she cried.

He looked very pleased with himself. 'Yes, classic tricks always appeal to an audience. But come closer, Jane. I want to involve you in the magic.'

She jumped up willingly and stood before him, feeling expectant.

'Hold out both your hands in front, and spread out your fingers. Concentrate on one of your fingers, but don't tell me which one, and don't give the game away with your eyes. Then, in a moment, I'll pick out the one you're thinking about.'

'You've got a ten-to-once chance of guessing correctly,' she told him.

'Those odds are too long for my liking. But, with the magic, I'm a certainty. . . Now, concentrate on the finger.'

She concentrated hard on her left index finger, and was careful not to look directly at it.

Then Dirk pressed his index finger gently down on each of her fingers. Miraculously, when he came to her chosen finger he said, 'This is the one, isn't it?'

'Yes! But how did you guess?' She was ecstatic, and smiled up wonderingly into his dark eyes.

'Your body told me,' was all the tantalising answer she received. 'Now I'd like to read directly into your mind.' He handed her a small white card and a pen. 'Put down a date that's important to you. Write it in block capitals. I'll turn my back so that there's no way I can see.'

Jane studied the ceiling for hidden mirrors, but she couldn't see any. She thought for a moment, and the first thing that came into her head was her birthday. But she dismissed the idea quickly. Most people would probably write that, and Dirk might have been able to find that out beforehand. So, to be a little tricky, she wrote, 'JANUARY 1ST', which actually had no significance other than the fact that it started the new year.

'Have you finished writing, Jane?'

'Yes.' She kept the card close against her chest.

Dirk turned swiftly and smiled directly into her eyes. 'Hold the card up, but keep it vertical so that I can't catch even a glimpse. . . That's it . . .perhaps a little higher, and keep your chin up.'

As he said this, he reached under the card and gently tapped her chin higher. 'That's right, just like that.'

Shutting his eyes tight, he appeared to be making a great mental effort. 'Yes. . .yes, your mind is becoming clear to me now. You've written January the first.'

Jane gasped, 'How did you do that?'

'By magic, of course.'

'Oh. . . I suppose you're going to keep all those secrets closely guarded, just like Harry Adamski. . . What else have you got in your repertoire. . .conjuring rabbits out of your top hat, or white doves from up your sleeve?'

'I'm not that advanced with magic,' he chuckled. 'Working with animals requires many years of dedicated practice, and you have to have a special affinity with those creatures.' He looked at her steadily. 'But I will reveal some secrets tonight, Jane. Let me start with the card tricks first. They rely on digital dexterity.'

He withdrew the Queen of Hearts from his top hat, and before her very eyes made the card appear and disappear within his hand.

'Slow down; I still can't work out exactly how you're doing that,' she laughed.

'In this trick, the quickness of the hand really does deceive the eye.' He performed the trick slowly over and over before her wondering face.

'That's so clever, Dirk. Let me try.'

With a hint of a smile, he handed over the card. But Jane fumbled the manoeuvre many times, and the card invariably ended up on the floor.

'This sort of manipulative magic is part of the repertoire of the professional gambler,' Dirk explained. 'But they also use prepared packs and specially printed cards. They have something in common with the conjurors, because they too use the psychology of deception and perception.'

'I don't like that association with conjuring,' Jane threw back. 'It makes it sound as if the conjurors are deceitful and underhand, yet all they do is entertain and give pleasure.'

'You may not like the idea, but I used deception and misdirection when I read your mind and the words you'd written on the card,' he told her.

He made her re-enact her exact movements for the trick, then he showed her the conjuror's simple technique. Jane felt deflated when the wonderful magic was revealed by realism.

Dirk watched her change of mood carefully. Then he picked up the white card with his three magic words and took her over to the chesterfield.

'Does this card still baffle you?' he asked.

She nodded.

'The riddle is very simple,' he began to explain. 'This is really one word, but it's been manipulated, and therefore your mind has been deceived. If you take out the spaces and read the word backwards, you'll see that the word is romance.' He produced a small flat mirror from a pocket.

He continued to speak solemnly as she stared at the card. 'You know I care very deeply about you, Jane. But sometimes your way of thinking causes me great worry.'

She lifted her eyes and looked at him curiously.

'I've practised for a long time to give you this supposedly impromptu magic night, because I wanted to show you that there's no mystery behind the magic. All the tricks you've seen here are based on certain knowledge, and nothing supernatural.'

Jane was dismayed to hear him talk like this, and she knew full well what he was driving towards.

'You must keep a sense of the realities, Jane. I don't mind you being superstitious about spilling salt on the table, but your ideas don't stop there.' He sighed. 'The other day when I was walking through the department I heard you telling a patient that some treatment was magic——'

'That must have been Harry Adamski,' she defended. 'And you know exactly why I should talk like that to him.'

'No, Jane.' His tone was stern. 'I don't know who the patient was, but it definitely wasn't Harry.'

She was bewildered; she couldn't think who he was talking about. In fact, she had completely forgotten about the fluorescent tube trick with Jake Malpass.

Dirk spoke rapidly now, ramming home his

points. 'You won't do the medical profession or yourself any favours by talking about magic. Some patients dream of instant and easy remedies. I've done some reading about Houdini, and I've found one such chilling example. Many people were so taken in by the great magician that they believed he had supernatural powers. Even the great actress Sarah Bernhardt, and she actually pleaded with him to restore her amputated leg.'

Now Jane was horrified. 'I've never put ideas like that into any patient's head. Such false hope would be cruel if nothing else.'

'But your mind has progressed on to more dangerous levels,' he persisted. 'The other day in the park, when we found Jill, you insisted that you'd had some premonition.'

Dirk had hit the raw nerve here. 'That was different!' she countered fiercely. 'I'll stand by my words now. I had a premonition then just as I had when my father died.'

'You must stop thinking like this.' She could hear that he was trying to keep the anger from his voice. 'I've gone to one hell of a lot of trouble tonight to prove to you that the "unknown" phenomena can all be explained. There's *nothing* supernatural.'

'Yes, there is!' she retaliated. 'I just know there is. And there are more things in heaven and earth than can be explained away by your science.'

He raked his hand through his hair and looked at her through intense eyes. 'Your persistent belief in the supernatural is at the core of this damnable conflict concerning my father. Can't you see? If you can't rid your mind of this nonsense, then. . .then it will always stand between resolving the grudge against my father, and. . .' he paused for effect '. . .and with coming to terms with your own father's death.'

Jane averted her face sharply and compressed her lips hard. She was nearly crying now. 'But science and an awareness of the unknown can work together——'

Two short rings on the intercom from the building's main entrance interrupted her sentence.

Dirk's eyes became even more narrow. He swivelled them towards the sound. 'That sounds like my father's ring, but——'

Jane's heart felt as though it would jump into her mouth. 'I can't meet him now. . .I'm not prepared. This isn't fair. . .you shouldn't have sprung this on me, Dirk.'

'Calm down, Jane.' He sounded het-up and irritated. 'It shouldn't be him. . .but if it is. . .' He looked at her intently.

The interrupting rings sounded again. Dirk jumped to his feet, and when the intercom conversation ended Jane sighed with relief. It had been a wrong enquiry.

Dirk leaned against the wall and she heard him exhale deeply. Then, turning slowly, he faced her square-on and spoke evenly.

'Well, you don't have to come face to face with your problem tonight, Jane.' The relief she felt was instant. 'But,' he continued, 'the love I have for my father is based on a blood bond. That'll never die. You know how I feel about you, but this conflict will tear us apart forever if it's not solved.'

Her eyes opened wider, and she listened even more intently.

'When my father returns from BC, he'll be here for a month. Now in that time our future will lie in your hands, Jane.'

'You're giving me an ultimatum,' she gulped.

'I have no choice,' he replied dully.

And Jane knew by the finality in his tone that he meant every word.

CHAPTER NINE

PASSION linked with pain had made Jane initially blind to the true, deep feelings behind Dirk's conjuring act. But, after reflecting on the whole evening, she knew he had acted out of deep love. She just had to get the courage to make her peace with his father. But she believed so ardently in her premonitions.

If Dirk's magic only stirred up turbulent emotions, then Harry Adamski's had been a resounding success.

During the hand class, Sister Veronica chatted on at great length. The children had been thrilled, and all the sisters at the convent entranced. And, as Jane watched the nun with light shining in her eyes, she was sure that when Harry packed up his conjuring tricks the magic still lived on for this lady.

But all was not well in Physiotherapy. The weather had turned into a scorching heat spell. The air-conditioning in the department was old and frequently needed attention. Claire Jousserand, the director, had summoned the engineers, and they had done their best with a temporary repair. However, as the machinery was old, they doubted that they could get spare parts if it broke down again, and so a whole new system would have to be installed.

Jane had one thing to be thankful about. She hadn't had a run-in with Jake Malpass, and this was due to one good reason. He hadn't shown up for his treatment again. She really ought to speak to Dirk about her awkward patient.

At the end of the day, when Jane was changing in the locker-room, Helen Davis said, 'I don't think I can face going home to my apartment right away. It faces south, and I forgot to draw the curtains this morning to keep the heat out. It'll be unbearable there.'

'My place will be stifling too,' Jane agreed. 'And I don't feel like cooking a thing.'

'The air-conditioning's always good in the Bay Restaurant downtown; why don't we go down there and do some shopping afterwards? The shops stay open late today,' Helen said.

'Great idea.'

The two set off for the restaurant, and after being revived with the cool air, and tuna salad and raspberries and cream, they wandered round the store.

Helen wanted to buy a new pair of jeans, because she was going trekking with her boyfriend in the mountains the following week. In the Jean Joint she chose several pairs and went to change in a cubicle. Jane took a close look at some blouses on display.

'Hi, Jane. I haven't seen you for ages.'

The voice sounded familiar, and Jane swivelled round to see a handsome upright young man, with warm smiling eyes.

'Hello, how are you?' She hid the uncertainty in her voice, as she searched his face. But, for the life of her, she couldn't place him. She couldn't remember treating him in the department, but on the weekends she had helped out on the wards, so she presumed he was probably a post-operative patient whom she had treated once to check his chest. Patients looked so different once they were out of a hospital bed.

'Swinging an axe with Uncle Chuck has made me fitter than I've ever been,' he told her.

'Yes, of course—Tom! I often wondered how you were getting on.' You could have knocked Jane down with a feather. Tom Gulliver looked so different, and calmly assured now.

'You've had your hair cut really short, just like Uncle Chuck,' she realised. 'It makes you look much older. . . No problems with your shoulder now, I hope?'

'None at all. Uncle Chuck and I have got a little business going now. It's a bit like your work, something like medicine.' Tom grinned broadly.

Whatever has he been up to? There's a joke coming, I think, Jane thought.

'We're tree surgeons,' he laughed. 'Well, not real surgeons, like Dr Blackwell. But we do lop and chop the limbs of trees. We've done quite a bit of work in our neighbourhood, and the money comes in useful. Mum's really happy.'

'Oh, I'm so glad for you, Tom,' said Jane.

'We had a careers counsellor at school,' he explained. 'And I'd like to stay working outdoors. I've decided to go into forestry, so I've got to work real hard at my studies and go to university.'

'That's a splendid idea, Tom. I think you'll do very well there too.'

'Sorry, I can't chat any more.' He checked his watch. 'I've got to get home for tea.'

'It's been great seeing you again,' Jane told him. They shook hands and said goodbye.

Jane could hardly believe the change in her old patient. Just then Helen came out of the cubicle and said, 'Goodness, he's changed! I remember him the first day he came for treatment, and you had to tell that story-line about the voodoo. No wonder you didn't recognise him at first.' She was thoughtful for a moment. 'You had another curious patient at that time too. Do you remember that guy you stretched so that he could enter the police?'

'Yes, Boyd Harvey. On the grapevine, I heard he'd been accepted. He must be finishing his initial training about now,' said Jane. 'I expect we'll walk out of this store and see him patrolling the streets in full uniform.'

'He won't have any problems,' Helen concluded. 'He didn't lack any confidence.'

Perhaps he had a little too much, thought Jane. But she dismissed the idea, and they went on with their shopping expedition.

At a quarter to eight the following morning Jane walked to work and looked up at the sky. A merciless sun blazed down, and there wasn't a cloud to be seen. It was going to be another scorcher.

Crossing her fingers as she entered through the main hospital doors, she hoped the air-conditioning was bearing up. But as the warm air of the physio department almost hit her she knew her hopes had been dashed.

Minutes later, when everyone from the out-patient team assembled in the office, Claire Jousserand entered, looking disgruntled.

'Hello, everyone,' she began. 'Well, I'm sorry to tell you it won't be a very comfortable day here. The engineers have promised to provide us with some temporary equipment to cool the department, but it has to come from another hospital, so they don't think they'll be able to get it set up and working until late this afternoon.'

Everyone groaned.

Claire continued, 'It's going to be far too hot for some of the heat treatments. We don't want anyone flaking out on us with heat stroke, so no short wave and no hot pack treatments today.'

Jane and the rest of the team found it difficult working through the heat. But all the patients were very understanding, and nobody complained.

But there were problems to come. And Helen brought the first to Jane later on, when the latter was cleaning out the leg whirlpool bath in the hydrotherapy section.

'Ah, so this is where you've been hiding,' Helen began. 'I've looked all over this place for you. Jake Malpass is here, and he's just complained to me that you're ten minutes late for his treatment.'

'Well, how kind of him to condescend to turn up for treatment,' Jane replied sarcastically.

'I know it's hot, and I know he's an everlasting nuisance, but I think it would be best to keep your cool with him today. He's got a nasty look about him. And in these sort of temperatures tempers can fly sky-high.'

'Thanks for reminding me, Helen.' Jane wiped the sweat from her brow with the back of her hand. 'I'll come straight away.'

She was as polite as she could be when she ushered Jake into a cubicle. 'I presume your back has been a problem again, Jake, so that was the reason you didn't turn up for treatment again?'

'It's been worse than ever,' he ground out. His eyes were narrow and he looked all set for a row. 'These treatments aren't doing me any good at all. I don't think it's good enough, and I've got a compensation board assessment later today.'

Ah, that's why he's put in an appearance today, thought Jane. She knew that if he didn't turn up for board assessments his claim would be put in jeopardy.

'I'm sorry we haven't been any help,' she tried to sound soothing, 'but if the short wave and the hot packs didn't work then we'll try something else today.'

'Glad to hear it,' he mumbled.

She made him comfortable on the plinth, then set off towards the ice machine. Perhaps a wet ice-pack would cool his temper. Some back patients swore by it. She shovelled the ice into a wet rectangular bag made of terry towel, then returned to her patient.

She spoke positively. 'A lot of patients, especially in this weather, find that if their tissues are cooled then a lot of the pain is eased. So let's try this.'

As soon as she placed the pack on his back, he let out a mighty groan. 'Oh, God! I might just as well go to the North Pole.'

'Try and relax, Jake,' she told him.

'It's damned freezing,' he shuddered, gritting his teeth together.

'As I said, try and relax—the ice will only stay on for twelve minutes for this first time.' Jane beat a hasty exit before he could start complaining again.

But she hadn't been in the office for five minutes when Helen dug her sharply in the ribs. Unfortunately, her friend's warning didn't come soon enough to give Jane any time to prepare for the wrath that was about to descend on her head.

Jake stood in the doorway, fully dressed, his face contorted and flaming red. He shook his forefinger at her. 'I've had enough of this place, and you, girl! You don't seem to know what you're doing. You're just using me as a guinea-pig. I've had a different treatment every time I've damn well come here. It's the same with those people at the Comp. Everybody's imcompetent!'

Jane was caught off guard by this outburst.

He raved on, 'I'm going to report you, girl! I'm going right up to Dr Blackwell's office, because I know he's there. And he's going to hear *all* about this. . . It's not my fault that my ribs grow into my hips.'

With this parting shot, he did a sharp about-turn that would have done any soldier on parade justice, and strode out of the department.

Helen and Jane burst out laughing.

Jane giggled. 'How can anybody's ribs grow into their hips?'

'I've never seen such an outrageous exhibition,' Helen agreed. 'But quick, Jane; you must ring Dirk Blackwell and warn him. Hurry up!' she urged. 'Dirk must be forewarned.'

But Helen was right. Jake was a nasty piece of work, and big with it. Suddenly the thought of Dirk in any sort of danger galvanised Jane into immediate action, and she grabbed the telephone and punched in his office number.

His secretary answered, and Jane had to concentrate to stop herself from gabbling. 'This is Jane Easter, from Physio. I'd like to speak to Dr Blackwell urgently, please.'

In moments she heard Dirk's voice. It sounded alert and concerned. 'What's the problem?' he asked.

'You've got a problem, and it's heading your way this very moment. Jake Malpass is in fighting mood. I'm pretty sure he's malingering to some extent, because his straight leg raise and Hoover tests bear this out. And, whatever I do, every single treatment makes him worse. Yet he was able to run out of the department like a wild bison——'

Dirk cut in, 'I distinctly remember giving that unpleasant character to Graham. I had no idea one of you girls would end up treating him.'

'Graham's on holiday; that's why I've inherited him. Oh, and Jake's got an anatomical anomaly that nobody seems to understand—his ribs grow into his hips!'

'Thanks for the warning. I'll get back to you.'

If Jane could have had one wish at that moment, she would have been a fly on the wall in that office. But she had to return to another patient.

However, it wasn't long before Helen found her and relayed the message that Dirk had rung back. Jane raced back, eager to hear the news.

'You were quite right to give me that warning call,' Dirk began. 'That frank malingerer came into my office with a stream of abuse that made the air blue. But I'd always suspected there was a large element of commercial malingering about him. So I gave him a swift treatment—a grade-four manipulation. I booted his backside all the way down the stairs.'

'I bet he wasn't expecting that reception,' Jane chuckled.

'Definitely not. But it was a very good test for back mobility. There was nothing patently wrong with Malpass, because he ran across the car park as if the very devil were behind him——' Dirk broke off suddenly. 'Sorry, I'm needed in Emergency——' The telephone clicked off.

Jane relayed the sequence of events to Helen, and they both held their thumbs in the air in triumph.

But, later on that afternoon, Jane caught sight of a very different Dirk as he marched towards Claire's office. He didn't notice Jane, because his face was a study of concentration, and he looked as though he were a black thundercloud about to burst.

Shortly afterwards, a pale and drained-looking Claire found Jane. 'Come into my office, please,' she said.

This must be something to do with Dirk's visit, thought Jane, and by the look on Claire's face it's a very serious matter.

'Shut the door behind you, and sit down,' the director began. She passed a nervous hand through her hair. 'I'm afraid I've just had some bad news. But whatever you feel, Jane, don't consider yourself to blame. I must shoulder that responsibility myself. Do you remember Boyd Harvey?'

A cold knot gripped Jane's stomach. 'Yes, I was only thinking about him the other day. He must have just completed his initial police training.'

Claire sighed. 'Yes, he was top in his class for all academic exams. But on his very first day on the streets he ran straight into deep trouble. Apparently he was with an older, more experienced policeman, and they found someone siphoning petrol from under a car. Against the older policeman's advice, Boyd rushed in and came off the worse, with knife wounds.'

'Oh, no.' Jane covered her mouth with her hand. That cavalier attitude she'd seen in the department had got him into trouble. 'How bad is he?'

'He's just come out of OR—apparently one of the knife wounds came within an inch of his heart. But he's stable and in Intensive Care now.'

Jane was shocked and silenced. She sat feeling very small and her mind was quite numb.

'It knocked the wind out of me too,' said Claire. 'I did have some reservations about taking Boyd on as a patient, but in the circumstances, and considering our code of ethics, I was wrong.'

She sighed, then continued, 'In Boyd's case, the outcome was almost fatal, so I shall write a memo on these lines to all the directors in the area. And I'll send another to the *Journal*.'

After studying Jane's face she said, 'I think you'd better go and have a cup of tea.'

But Jane went straight back to her work, pushing the sequence of events out of her mind. But she felt like an automaton even as she walked home.

From out of nowhere came a voice. 'Slow down, Jane. I had to call you twice.' Dirk ran up from behind.

Then she remembered that he was the doctor who had refused to refer Boyd for physio. And it must have been Dirk, with that thunderous face, who had told Claire the bad news.

'Oh, no,' she sighed wearily. 'The last thing I need right now is you telling me you were right about Boyd, especially on top of everything else.'

'Absolutely right, and I'm not going to do anything of the sort.' He slid his arm about her shoulder. 'Now you come up to my apartment, because you look as if you're in shock.'

In the sitting-room, he handed her a glass of brandy. 'Here, drink this. It's medicinal.'

'Thank you.' She took the glass and sipped slowly. He sat close by her side on the chesterfield. 'I suppose you were in Emergency when Boyd came in this afternoon,' she said.

'Yes, and by the look on his face he won't be in a hurry to put on that uniform again.'

Jane clasped her glass with both hands and stared down at the amber fluid. 'It's all my fault he's in hospital now,' she sobbed. 'I worked and worked on him, and it was only by chance that he made the height. He was four millimetres short, but I saw Graham reading a book on the foot, and using a postcard of a bridge as a marker. And that's where I got the idea of teaching Boyd to use his lumbricals, and artificially grow. . . I've been caught up in a cruel twist of fate.'

'Nonsense,' he said firmly but kindly, pulling her closer to his side. 'You weren't a part of fate. Boyd joined the police through his own free will, because he chose to take up the job.' Then he added in an undertone, 'Or, at least, his father did.'

He continued in more soothing tones, 'You were only doing your job, Jane, carrying out orders. And, as usual, you thought out your treatment intelligently. Now, no more talk of fate—and definitely don't blame yourself.'

He took the glass from her trembling hands and placed it to one side on a table. Then he pulled her on to his lap.

She slid her arms about him, and in the perfect and natural silence she felt his kind words dispelling all her guilt.

Dirk said nothing, but continued to softly stroke her hair. She relaxed further against his body, and her mind began to float. Here was the one man in the world whom she desired, the one man she loved. By his side she felt so right.

'Let's get more comfortable, sweetheart.' Dirk eased her off his lap so that they were lying. The full length of his body was now pressed close up against hers, and she thrilled to his rock-hardness. The sensations in her body wiped out everything else.

At first his kisses were gentle and delicate, but as she began to respond more ardently his tongue sought hers and probed her mouth.

'I've wanted you for such a long, long time.' He sounded husky.

His skilful hands eased her aching breasts free from the confines of her clothes, and his tongue sent delicious flickers of shuddering sensations coursing through her veins.

Small half-caught sounds of murmuring delight escaped her. No man had ever had this effect on her before. Her feelings grew in intensity, so that she felt she desired nothing else in the world. She could feel his muscles judder under her caress.

Then, as if the magic build-up was being tantalisingly withdrawn, he rolled off. Flushed and still aroused, she turned to him, and saw a monumental tension on his face. She was half afraid.

Then he caught her roughly to him, and, holding her as if in a vice, whispered raggedly, 'After this business with Boyd, can't you see how destructive this belief in fate and the supernatural is?'

Jane was shocked into silence.

He continued, his voice thick with emotion but low, 'Relinquish all your supernatural beliefs, Jane. Do it now. . .and then promise me we can fix a date to talk with my father.'

The emotions of her highly aroused desires overflowed and flared into temper.

'You bastard! You think you can excite me and use sex to make me agree to anything.' She was furious.

Gripping her shoulders, he held her captive. 'Sometimes you're so stupid, Jane. How can I be using sex when I've pulled up short? For

God's sake, it's precisely because I care, precisely because I want you for more than your body, that I'm acting like this.'

They were both shaking with anger now.

'This upset over Boyd only proves my point further. Can't you see reason, Jane?'

She read the desperate concern in his eyes, and it touched her soul.

'I love you,' he said softly. 'For God's sake, this must be sorted now.'

She was quiet and withdrawn for a moment, as she stared at the tufts of hair on his chest.

'I will meet your father. . .' she began. He held her tighter and sighed deeply. 'But,' she continued, 'I still believe in the unknown and premonitions. And I've got the most terrible feeling that you'll only meet me halfway when one of my premonitions comes true.'

He sat up jerkily, glaring darkly. 'There seems to be no solution to all this, Jane. But my father will be here for a few weeks. . .and when that time is up our relationship will be sealed one way or another!'

CHAPTER TEN

Jane's night back in her own apartment was anything but restful and peaceful. Her last encounter with Dirk made that impossible. And pressing into her mind came images of darkness and danger.

At six-thirty in the morning she sat bolt upright in bed, drenched in a cold sweat. The identity of the man in distress had clearly been revealed in her mind's eye. It had been Dirk.

It's a premonition, for sure, she thought. I must warn him.

Shakily she climbed out of bed and headed for the telephone in the next room. But annoyingly it rang and rang, and still nobody answered.

Perhaps he's been called in, and he's at the hospital, she thought. So she decided to make a very early start at work so that she could check up on him.

At seven o'clock she was walking purposefully up to the main entrance of the hospital, when she spotted Dirk in the foyer. She ran in breathlessly and dragged him to a secluded corner. 'Thank God you're here. I've been so worried about you!' she exclaimed.

'You look worse than I feel, Jane. Have you had any constructive thoughts about last night?'

She ignored this. 'I've hardly slept a wink, because I've had these terrible recurring. . .' She hesitated to say the word premonitions. 'Recurring nightmares.' She came straight to the point. 'You must take great care, especially when it's dark. I've had the overwhelming feeling that something awful is about to happen to you.'

'I'm perfectly safe—you can see for yourself,' he answered coolly.

'Maybe not this minute, but some time in the future.'

He looked weary, then a jaded expression crossed his face. 'Not one of your premonitions, Jane? I'm big enough to take care of myself.'

She felt as if he were humouring her, as if she were a child, and this angered her. Last night boiled up in her mind. 'You must take this seriously. I believe you could be in grave danger in a dark place.'

'I like your concern, sweetheart, and to put your mind at rest I'll pick you up at seven-thirty tonight for supper. Then, later on, you can take me back to your place and keep a very close eye on me until the dawn breaks.' His tone was cutting.

'Then I'll keep you every night. Yes, I believe in this so strongly.'

He raised both eyebrows this time. 'You'll

make a masterful mistress, Jane. I can hardly
wait to see how you put me through my paces
in the bedroom.'

'You flippant, stupid man!' she almost hissed.
'This is something far more important than sex.
This is something terrible and deadly. . .I just
know it.'

'If these premonitions of yours are so fool-
proof, why didn't you warn Boyd Harvey?'

Damn his logical scientific mind, she thought
desperately. 'I did think of Boyd, and only the
day before his terrible attack, but I don't get
these deep specific feelings about everyone.'

Dirk sighed audibly as if tired of the argument. 'Relax, Jane; nothing's going to happen
to me. I'll pick you up at seven-thirty tonight.'

But she wasn't pacified, and her feelings of
imminent danger began to increase as the day
wore on.

One incident shone a light into her dark,
sombre mood. The physio from Intensive Care
told her that Boyd was well out of danger, and
that it was only a matter of time now for him to
recover completely.

Towards the end of the afternoon she felt
thirsty, so she went to the little shop in the
hospital to buy orange juice. There it came as a
surprise that she had just enough money. She
would have to go to the bank directly after
work.

The nearest branch was slightly out of her

way, and after collecting some money she had to walk an unusual way home. It would be quicker if she took a short cut between the blocks, so she headed out down a dusty back alley.

Because this part of Canada was literally covered in ice and snow for five months or more of the year, many builders were taking advantage of the summer weather. Ahead, a row of houses had been demolished to make way for a block of apartments. The company had taken all the necessary precautions by boarding the area up and putting up warning signs.

But in several places Jane could see that the boards had been wrenched away, giving easy access for intruders. As she passed she glimpsed the huge excavating machines. Now, after the day's work, they stood still and silent like gigantic metal monsters. They fascinated her, and she thought they would be even more fascinating to a child.

Suddenly she became fiercely anxious. She stopped dead in her tracks as if a suffocating blackness descended all around her. She shook off the feeling and opened her eyes wide to scan the area.

Then inside her head she heard a terrified loud cry for help. As if homing in like a laser, she sprinted round the corner, and without knowing why she ducked through an opening in the boards. Running full pelt, she headed towards a trench.

It looked as if the sides had only recently collapsed. And there, thrust through the earth, she could just make out a man's wrist and hand. The fingers were spread wide as if desperately reaching out for help.

She heard that voice again in her head, but this time definitely muffled and fainter.

'I'm coming, Dirk!' she shouted, and sprinted madly to the spot. Although she felt an intense feeling of panic, she knew that a high-speed, quality-thinking response was needed here.

'Hold on, Dirk!' she commanded, as she scooped the earth away from his arm, then dug down frantically like a terrier.

Quickly she scooped away great mounds of earth, and at last came to his head. With lightning fingers she cleared away the dirt from his eyes and nostrils and mouth.

'Open your eyes—open your eyes,' she said firmly. She didn't like the colour of his face.

She knew he had a body of flexible steel like Houdini, but she was sure her man didn't possess the master magician's secrets that enabled him to escape being buried alive.

Her heart was beating frantically in her chest, because she couldn't see any signs of breathing. 'Breathe—take deep breaths, Dirk.'

After an agonising time while she continued

to excavate his torso, his eyes flickered open, and he spat out some dirt.

'What kept you, Jane? I had to call twice.'

'Oh, you beloved bastard!' Tears began to prick her eyes.

'There's a little guy under all this somewhere,' he added.

From nowhere several men rushed up. 'The ambulance is coming,' someone told her. Then they gathered round to help.

'Be careful how you dig him out,' Jane cautioned. 'He might have fractured ribs. . .'

The men soon had Dirk free and then went on to find the boy. Jane supervised Dirk's lifting, so that if an injury had occurred nothing more dangerous would complicate matters. And she sat by his side, holding his hand tight.

She heard the ambulance siren wail nearer, and soon the paramedics were on the scene. She helped transfer Dirk on to a stretcher and then into the back of the vehicle.

One of the men said, 'Lucky thing an older lady from the apartments saw you rush up and start digging. She told the caretaker, who organised us to come.'

'Thank God for that,' Jane said. 'Every second counts in situations like these. Thank you all.'

The sequence of events that followed in the hospital flashed by blurringly fast. The boy recovered consciousness and was taken to X-ray, and Dirk also had films taken which fortunately checked out OK, and he was admitted to a single room on the trauma ward.

When they were alone together, Dirk said, 'I've got something very important to tell you, sweetheart.'

'You don't have to talk now,' she told him, 'just rest.'

'No, I want to tell you. . . I never believed anything that couldn't be explained by science, let alone your premonitions. But now I do. . . and that's because I'm alive.'

'I heard your telepathic cry for help,' she explained. 'It was the strangest thing, because normally I would never have been in that vicinity.'

He squeezed her hand. 'And it was your talk about Houdini that helped me to hang on until you came. I'd done some reading on the man, and I remembered he said that panic was a dangerous thing. So I tried to preserve a calmness of spirit, and that helped me eke out the air in my lungs.'

'So the master's magic lives again,' she sighed softly.

A nurse and an older man entered the room. 'Your father is here to see you, Dr Blackwell,' the woman said.

Jane was sitting with her back to the cardiologist at this point.

'How are you feeling now, son?' The elder Dr Blackwell strode up to the bed.

'A bit bruised. But I'm here to tell the tale, thanks to Jane here.' Dirk made the introductions.

Panic gripped her heart. Dirk looked her steadily in the eyes, and she knew he was silently saying, I love you desperately, Jane. But now you must choose.

Steeling her every nerve and screwing up her courage, Jane turned slowly to see her old acquaintance. She must be strong for Dirk. And suddenly she knew she could be. It did not matter if Dr Blackwell senior had refused to listen to her. He had cared for her father to the best of his ability, and some things were just meant to be. Nearly losing Dirk had shown her both how empty her life would be without him and that her father's counselling against revenge was right.

She looked up into the older doctor's face and astonishment made her eyes grow wide. The kindness on Dr Blackwell's face was unmistakable as he took her hand firmly between his.

'Thank you so much, my dear. I can never say or do enough to repay you for saving my son's life. I do hope that we can now be friends, because Dirk never stops talking about you.'

Jane swallowed hard. 'I'm so glad. . .' These were all the words she could manage before great tears started to roll down her cheeks.

'There, there, my dear. . .' Dr Blackwell slid

his arm about her shoulder. 'The full impact of everything has only just caught up on you.'

She wept freely, and hugged the older man tightly. Dr Blackwell spoke to his son for only a short while, then discreetly excused himself and left.

When doctor and physio were alone, Jane took a deep breath, only to have Dirk pull her close.

'I can see from your face, my darling, that you have come to terms with what happened to your father. Do you think you can learn to love my father as I do? He can never replace your own, but I think you will find he is anxious to accept you as a daughter.'

Jane sighed with relief, and smiled radiantly.

'Oh, yes,' she said, with utter conviction.

The following evening, after a hastily made supper, Jane was preparing to go back to the hospital to visit Dirk again. They had had precious little time alone together. Suddenly, an imperious knock sounded on her apartment door. The visitor on the other side was the last man she expected to see.

'Dirk, you shouldn't be out of hosptial, let alone out of bed!' she exclaimed.

'Don't forget I'm a doctor, Jane. I'm fully competent to make a clinical decision about my discharge. But about the other. . .well, perhaps you're right.'

'Be serious,' she laughed, and pulled him inside.

He closed the door smartly, and pulled her into his arms. His kisses were deep and passionate. They clung to each other then, locked in such a tight embrace that neither wanted to let the other go.

Jane gripped Dirk even tighter and pressed her cheek hard against his chest. 'I've been such a fool,' she began. 'I almost lost you. And you know, my father was right all along. He warned me not to pursue any sort of revenge, because he said I'd be the only one to get hurt. . . If you left me then a part of my heart would be dead forever.'

Dirk spoke softly into her ear. 'All that matters is that we're together now. We've both learned a lot. Revenge only hurts itself, and I think you know that now.'

She nodded.

He continued, 'Don't forget I learnt something too, Jane. When you heard my telepathic cry for help, I became a believer in the unknown.'

She looked up into his brilliant sparkling eyes.

Then he continued, 'I agree, sweetheart, there are more things in heaven and earth then we can rationalise away. . .except one thing. . .'

She frowned at him quizzically.

'I'll show you in the bedroom.' His grin

widened as he picked her up, and immediately strode through the correct door. 'I promise you one thing—our lovemaking will be fun, beautiful, and fulfilling. And that's the way it will always be.'

By the bed he deliberately tugged her blouse free from the waistband of her skirt, then expertly flicked her buttons undone, starting from below and working upwards. He eased the soft material over her shoulders and let the garment slide to the floor.

When his gaze met hers, she saw the flash of desire light up his eyes, and an answering flame kindled deep within her body.

She reached up and unknotted his tie, her movements clumsy in her haste to know him fully. Dirk stayed her hand and kissed her fingertips reverently.

'We'll take our time. . .' He spoke softly but with a huskiness that made his voice deep.

But his slow and more deliberate movements as they undressed only made Jane more excited. His eyes were fixed on her intently as he discarded the remainder of his clothes. She loved the powerful masculine lines of his lean body, so different from the soft curves of her own.

He folded back the bedclothes and lifted her in, then quickly slid by her side. He gathered her close, and the warmth of his body roused her, and the heat of his potent manhood sent waves of molten desire coursing through her veins.

Dirk covered her mouth with his and kissed her hungrily. She felt the quickening throb of his desire throughout his entire body, and she thought he would take her then and there in his haste. But he eased his weight away and began to delicately explore her body with his lips and tongue and fingers. .

She marvelled at his masterful control, and the way he held his body in check. The tenderness of his touch made her tremble as his hand moved lower to excite her most intimate, secret places.

Her hands explored his body, delighting in the contrast of his rock-hard muscles, the flare of the bone at his hips and the velvet texture of his potency.

He whispered words of love and endearment, and other words that heightened her response, as he brought her to ever-increasing pitches of pleasure. These built into shuddering waves of ecstasy. She thought she would die in his arms of a surfeit of pure pleasure.

As he worked her desire to a more frantic level, she was only barely conscious of the fact that the sheer effort he had to make to hold back was monumental, and when he pressed into her she gasped and shuddered more deeply than ever. Soon all control was beyond him, as his need for her increased, and she felt his first sharp ecstasy inside her. But she loved her man so much that she took all of him and gloried in his deepest love touch.

When their breathing became calmer, she soothed him with her trembling fingertips, and pushed his sweat-drenched hair from his forehead.

'Body magic with you is the best in the world,' she said, feeling slightly in awe.

His emerald eyes were dreamy and smiling. 'That's the way it should be, my love. . . I might not be Houdini with a magic wand up my sleeve——'

She placed her forefinger over his lips. 'I had noticed that you didn't keep it there. . .'

He chuckled deep in his throat. 'You're a young madam. . .and you've got a wicked sense of humour. And I love you all the more for it.'

'I love you too,' she whispered softly against his mouth.

They slept the deep sleep of satisfied lovers, facing each other and locked tightly together, and there they remained fused and bonded with each other in every sense. And these feelings were only intensified as they made love many more times.

If Jane and Dirk had any further ability with extra-sensory perception then they would have looked into the near future and seen two of their patients. On the convent steps, Mother Superior and the rest of the nuns would wave Sister Veronica goodbye. And watch her as she and Harry Adamski set off for a new life together.

— MEDICAL ✓ ROMANCE —

The books for enjoyment this month are:

BEYOND HEAVEN AND EARTH Sara Burton
SISTER AT HILLSIDE Clare Lavenham
IN SAFE HANDS Margaret O'Neill
STORM IN PARADISE Judith Worthy

♥   ♥   ♥   ♥   ♥

Treats in store!

Watch next month for the following absorbing stories:

PLAYING THE JOKER Caroline Anderson
ROMANCE IN BALI Margaret Barker
SURGEON'S STRATEGY Drusilla Douglas
HEART IN JEOPARDY Patricia Robertson

Available from Boots, Martins, John Menzies, W.H. Smith, most supermarkets and other paperback stockists.

Also available from Mills & Boon Reader Service, P.O. Box 236, Thornton Road, Croydon, Surrey CR9 3RU.

Readers in South Africa - write to:
Book Services International Ltd, P.O. Box 41654, Craighall, Transvaal 2024.

Mills & Boon

Four brand new romances from favourite
Mills & Boon authors have been specially
selected to make your Christmas special.

THE FINAL SURRENDER
Elizabeth Oldfield

SOMETHING IN RETURN
Karen van der Zee

HABIT OF COMMAND
Sophie Weston

CHARADE OF THE HEART
Cathy Williams

Published in November 1992   Price: £6.80

Mills & Boon

Discover the thrill of 4 Exciting Medical Romances – FREE

FREE

BOOKS FOR YOU

In the exciting world of modern medicine, the emotions of true love have an added drama. Now you can experience four of these unforgettable romantic tales of passion and heartbreak FREE – and look forward to a regular supply of Mills & Boon Medical Romances delivered direct to your door!

❧ ❧ ❧

Turn the page for details of 2 extra free gifts, and how to apply.

An Irresistible Offer from Mills & Boon

Here's an offer from Mills & Boon to become a regular reader of Medical Romances. To welcome you, we'd like you to have four books, a cuddly teddy and a special MYSTERY GIFT, all absolutely free and without obligation.

Then, every month you could look forward to receiving 4 more **brand new** Medical Romances for £1.60 each, delivered direct to your door, post and packing free. Plus our newsletter featuring author news, competitions, special offers, and lots more.

This invitation comes with no strings attached. You can cancel or suspend your subscription at any time, and still keep your free books and gifts.

Its so easy. Send no money now. Simply fill in the coupon below and post it at once to -

**Mills & Boon Reader Service, FREEPOST,
PO Box 236, Croydon, Surrey CR9 9EL**

NO STAMP REQUIRED

- -

YES! Please rush me my 4 Free Medical Romances and 2 Free Gifts! Please also reserve me a Reader Service Subscription. If I decide to subscribe, I can look forward to receiving 4 brand new Medical Romances every month for just £6.40, delivered direct to my door. Post and packing is free, and there's a free Mills & Boon Newsletter. If I choose not to subscribe I shall write to you within 10 days - I can keep the books and gifts whatever I decide. I can cancel or suspend my subscription at any time. I am over 18.

EP20D

Name (Mr/Mrs/Ms) _____

Address _____

_____

_____ Postcode _____

Signature _____